'The house only has two bedrooms.'

'Then I guess I'll have to share with you.'

'I'd rather share my bed with the devil,' Kristen said tartly, desperate to disguise the ache of tears in her voice as she was overwhelmed by memories of the past.

Sergio's brows rose. 'I didn't get that impression on Friday night.'

She flushed. 'That was a mistake.'

'In that case my experiment should reveal the truth.'

Kristen had not been aware of Sergio moving, but suddenly he was far too close for comfort. And as he reached behind her and cupped the nape of her neck she realised too late that she had walked into a trap.

'Don't...' Her voice faltered as his head swooped and his warm breath feathered her lips.

'I am about to prove that you are a little liar, *cara*,' he th_____ _____ _____ before __ st___led her prote___

THE BOND OF BROTHERS

Bound by blood, separated by secrets

Dark, powerful and devastatingly handsome,
the Castellano brothers have fought much to overcome
their difficult childhood—but separation and secrets
have left their scars.

Now these two men must ensure that their children
do not inherit their painful legacy…

This month read Sergio's story in:
HIS UNEXPECTED LEGACY

Read Salvatore's story in
SECRETS OF A POWERFUL MAN
November 2013

HIS UNEXPECTED LEGACY

BY
CHANTELLE SHAW

First published in Great Britain 2013
by Mills & Boon, an imprint of Harlequin (UK) Limited.
Harlequin (UK) Limited, Eton House, 18-24 Paradise Road,
Richmond, Surrey TW9 1SR

© Chantelle Shaw 2013

ISBN: 978 0 263 90042 2

Harlequin (UK) policy is to use papers that are natural, renewable and recyclable products and made from wood grown in sustainable forests. The logging and manufacturing process conform to the legal environmental regulations of the country of origin.

Printed and bound in Spain
by Blackprint CPI, Barcelona

Chantelle Shaw lives on the Kent coast, five minutes from the sea, and does much of her thinking about the characters in her books while walking on the beach. An avid reader from an early age, her school friends used to hide their books when she visited, but Chantelle would retreat into her own world, and still writes 'stories' in her head all the time.

Chantelle has been blissfully married to her own tall, dark and very patient hero for over twenty years, and has six children. She began to read Mills & Boon® as a teenager, and throughout the years of being a stay-at-home mum to her brood found romantic fiction helped her to stay sane!

Her aim is to write books that provide an element of escapism, fun, and of course romance for the countless women who juggle work and home life and who need their precious moments of 'me' time. She enjoys reading and writing about strong-willed, feisty women and even stronger-willed sexy heroes. Chantelle is at her happiest when writing. She is particularly inspired while cooking dinner, which unfortunately results in a lot of culinary disasters! She also loves gardening, taking her very badly behaved terrier for walks and eating chocolate (followed by more walking—at least the dog is slim!).

Recent titles by the same author:

CAPTIVE IN HIS CASTLE
AT DANTE'S SERVICE
THE GREEK'S ACQUISITION
BEHIND THE CASTELLO DOORS

**Did you know these are also available as eBooks?
Visit www.millsandboon.co.uk**

CHAPTER ONE

EARL'S DAUGHTER BAGS Sicilian Billionaire!

The lurid tabloid headline caught Kristen's attention as she hurried past the newspaper kiosk at Camden Town tube station. Maybe it was the word *Sicilian* that made her stop and buy a copy of the paper, although it did not cross her mind that the headline could be referring to Sergio. It was only when she had jammed herself into a packed train carriage and managed to unfold the paper that she saw his photograph—and for a few seconds her heart stopped beating. Conflicting emotions surged through her as she stared at the image of her son's father. She had not expected Nico to bear such a strong resemblance to Sergio but the likeness between the three-year-old boy and the swarthy Sicilian was uncanny.

Kristen's first instinct was to tear her eyes from the page but curiosity compelled her to study the photograph and the caption beneath it:

Lady Felicity Denholm was spotted with her new fiancé, Italian business tycoon Sergio Castellano, when the couple visited the London Palladium earlier this week.

The text beside the picture continued:

Earl Denholm is reported to be delighted that his youngest daughter is to marry one of Italy's richest men. The Castellano Group owns a chain of luxury hotel and leisure complexes around the world. Sergio heads the property development side of the business, while his twin brother Salvatore runs the family's world-famous vineyards at the Castellano estate in Sicily.

Wedged between a businessman wielding a large briefcase and a teenager wearing an enormous backpack, Kristen gripped the support rail as the train picked up speed. It was becoming something of a habit to learn of Sergio's marriage plans in the press, she thought bitterly. She remembered how shocked and hurt she had felt four years ago when she had read about his engagement to a beautiful Sicilian woman, barely two months after their relationship had ended. Presumably his first marriage had not lasted long if he was now about to marry a member of the English aristocracy.

In the photograph Felicity Denholm was clinging to Sergio's arm and wore the triumphant smile of a cat that had drunk all the cream, Kristen noted sourly. Sergio was even more stunningly good-looking than he had been four years ago. His black tuxedo moulded his broad shoulders and emphasised his powerful physique. But it was his face that trapped Kristen's attention. Blessed with a perfectly chiselled bone-structure, his features were leaner than she remembered. Harder. And, although in the picture he was smiling, nothing could detract from the implacable resoluteness of his jaw.

He was a man who knew his own mind and who pursued his goals with ruthless determination, proclaimed his dark, curiously expressionless eyes. They appeared to be black, but Kristen knew that his eyes were actually the colour of bitter chocolate and could, on rare occasions, soften and invite you to drown in their depths.

Memories flooded her mind of the golden summer she had spent in Sicily four years ago. She had met Sergio soon after she had arrived and the attraction between them had been instant and electrifying. She remembered the first time he had kissed her. They had been talking and laughing together, when he had suddenly dipped his head and brushed his mouth across hers. Even now, the memory was so intense that her stomach clenched. The kiss had been so beautiful and she had realised at that moment that she was in love. Foolishly, she had believed that Sergio shared the sentiment, but for him she had simply been a fleeting diversion from his jet-setting lifestyle.

It was a relief when the train pulled into Tottenham Court Road station and she shoved the newspaper into her bag as she was swept along with the throng of commuters towards the escalator. But the leaden sensation in Kristen's chest remained when she reached the street, and a few minutes later she walked through the doors of Fast-track Sports Physiotherapy Clinic and was greeted with a concerned look from her boss, Stephanie Bower.

'I take it from your expression that Nico didn't want to go to day-care again?' Steph's eyes narrowed on Kristen's tense face. 'Or are you ill? You look like you've seen a ghost.'

'Actually, I've seen Nico's father.' The words spilled from Kristen before she could prevent them, the sense of shock that still gripped her causing her to abandon her usual reticence about her private life.

Steph emitted a low whistle. 'No way? I thought you'd

had no contact with him since Nico was born. Where did you see him?' She stared at the newspaper Kristen handed her.

'That's him, Nico's father,' Kristen said flatly, pointing to the photo on the front page.

'Sergio Castellano! You're kidding, right?' Steph's eyebrows disappeared beneath her fringe when Kristen shook her head. 'Jeez—you're not kidding. But how on earth did you ever get mixed up with a drop-dead sexy, hotshot playboy? Not that I'm surprised,' she added hastily. 'Let's face it, you're a gorgeous blonde and you were bound to catch his attention. But you are a physiotherapist living in Camden and he's a billionaire who likes to cruise around the Med on a luxury yacht the size of the QE2. Where did you meet him?'

'In Sicily,' Kristen sighed. 'I'd taken a gap year from university to concentrate on trying to win a gold medal at the gymnastics world championships, but I had a bad bout of flu and fell behind with my training. My GP suggested I should go somewhere warm for a while to recuperate. My stepfather, who was also my coach, had a friend who owned a villa in Sicily which happened to have a gym. Alan rented the villa for six months, and he, Mum and I flew out there. But soon after we arrived my mum and stepdad had to return to England because Alan's father had died unexpectedly.

'I remained in Sicily.' Kristen gave a rueful smile. 'It was the first time I'd ever lived on my own. Even though I was studying at university, I still lived at home so that I could follow Alan's strict training schedule. I loved gymnastics, but I had started to feel that it had taken over my life. I'd never even had a proper boyfriend. I guess that's why I was swept off my feet by Sergio,' she said heavily. 'The Castellano estate was close to the villa where I was staying. I quite literally ran into Sergio one day on the beach and he was so sexy and charming that I was blown away by him. I couldn't believe my luck that he seemed to be attracted to me.'

She grimaced. 'I was very naïve. My stepfather was a dominant figure in my life and he was determined that I would be a top gymnast. I'd had a sheltered upbringing, but suddenly I was free from Alan's influence and I rushed headlong into an affair with Sergio.'

Steph gave her a speculative look. 'But at the end of the summer I suppose you had to return to England, and you came home with more than just a suntan,' she murmured. 'I assume you fell pregnant with Nico while you were in Sicily? Didn't Castellano offer to support you when you told him you were expecting his baby? What a bastard, especially when he's loaded…'

'I didn't tell him.' Kristen interrupted Steph before she could launch into one of her feminist diatribes against the male species. Fresh from an acrimonious divorce after discovering that her husband who she had adored was a serial adulterer, Steph's opinion of men was that they should all be boiled in oil.

'Sergio doesn't know about Nico. He made it very clear during our affair that he wasn't looking for a committed relationship of any kind, and I knew when I found out I was pregnant that he wouldn't be interested in his child.'

The full truth of what had happened four years ago was too complicated to explain, and too painful for Kristen to want to dwell on. Often when she looked at Nico she thought about the other baby she had lost and felt an ache of sadness. Forcing her mind from the past, she saw that Steph was concentrating on the newspaper article.

'So Nico's filthy-rich father is getting married to a spoiled socialite, and it says here that the couple will share their time between his home in Sicily, a luxury apartment in Rome and the multi-million pound house that Sergio is currently buying on Park Lane. That's when he and the lovely Lady Felicity aren't aboard his yacht or travelling on his private jet,' Steph said sardonically. 'Meanwhile you are struggling to bring up Castellano's son alone, with no financial help. It's outrageously unfair.'

Kristen shrugged. 'I'm not struggling,' she murmured, unaware of the weariness in her voice. The salary she earned as a physiotherapist covered her mortgage and bills, and although it was true that the cost of living seemed to have rocketed recently she was still able to provide Nico with everything he needed. 'It's true I can't go mad with money, but who can at the moment?'

Steph dropped the newspaper onto her desk and gave Kristen a rueful look. 'I know you're finding things more difficult now that you have to pay childcare costs since your mum died. But I'm not just talking about the fact that you are struggling financially. You're still grieving for Kathleen, and so is Nico. It's the reason he's been so clingy lately and why he cries every time you leave him at nursery.'

'His nursery worker says he stops crying after I've gone,' Kristen muttered tightly. She knew Steph was simply showing friendly concern, but she felt guilty enough about leaving Nico, and the sound of his sobs as she had walked out of the day-care centre this morning had made her feel as if her heart was being ripped out. 'What do you suggest I do? I would love to stay at home with Nico like my mum did, but I'm a single mother and I have no choice but to go to work.'

'I think you need to take a sabbatical,' Steph said firmly. 'I wouldn't be saying this if I wasn't so worried about you. Heaven knows, you're a valuable member of staff.

But I can see you're close to the edge. You need to take a couple of months off while you try and come to terms with losing your mum, and so that you can be a full-time mum to Nico.'

Tears filled Kristen's eyes as she thought of her mother. Kathleen had moved in with her when she'd given birth to Nico and had looked after him when Kristen had returned to work. The accident five months ago had been such a terrible shock. Kathleen had popped to the shops because they had run out of milk and been hit by a speeding car as she had crossed the road. She had been killed instantly, the policewoman who had broken the news had explained. Kristen was thankful that her mum hadn't suffered, but Steph was right, she hadn't come to terms with the tragedy and her grief was made worse because she knew that Nico desperately missed his beloved Nana.

She sighed. 'It's a nice idea, but I can't give up work. I'd have to win the Lottery first.'

'Here's your ticket.' Steph picked up the newspaper and jabbed her finger at Sergio's handsome face. 'It's only fair that Nico's father should take some responsibility for his son.'

'*No!*' Kristen said so fiercely that Steph gave her a curious look. 'I told you, Sergio is unaware of Nico's existence. And if he knew he had a child he wouldn't want anything to do with him. I'm certainly not going to ask him for money.'

'I'm not suggesting you demand a massive maintenance agreement,' Steph argued. 'You simply want a bit of financial help for a couple of months so that you can give Nico the care and attention he needs right now.'

'My son is my responsibility,' Kristen said in a tone that warned her friend to drop the subject. But she had to admit that Steph had made a valid point when she'd said that Nico was in need of extra care to help him deal with the loss of his grandmother. He might only be three years old, but Kristen didn't underestimate his grief. Over the past few months he had grown pale and listless and his lack of appetite was worrying.

'Give him time,' Kristen's GP had advised. 'Nico gets upset when you leave him at nursery because he's afraid, quite naturally under the circumstances, that you won't come back. Gradually he will come to accept the death of his grandmother. All you can do is to give him plenty of love and reassurance.'

She would love to rent a cottage by the sea for the summer and take Nico away for a holiday, Kristen thought wistfully. But it was impossible. The mortgage on her house would not pay itself. She pushed thoughts of the past away and forced herself to concentrate on her appointments. In her job she treated patients with a wide variety of sport-related injuries and usually she found the work absorbing. But today the clinic dragged, and even during the Pilates class she ran later in the day her mind was distracted and for once she was glad when the session was over.

The Tube was as busy at the height of the evening rush-hour as it had been in the morning but luckily there were no delays on her line and she was on time to collect Nico. He was waiting with the other children, his eyes fixed on the door as the parents filed into the nursery, and the moment he caught sight of Kristen his face lit up with a smile that tugged on her heart.

'Mummy!' He hurtled across the room and into her arms.

'Hello, Tiger. Have you had a nice day?'

Nico did not reply, but as Kristen lifted him up he linked his arms around her neck and pressed his face into her shoulder. His hair smelled of baby shampoo and felt like silk against her cheek. He was the most precious thing in her life and the intensity of her love for him brought a lump to her throat.

'I missed you.' Eyes as round and dark as chocolate buttons looked at her from beneath long, curling lashes. Nico's eyes were the exact same shade as his father's. The thought slid into Kristen's mind as she recalled the photo in the paper of Sergio and she felt a knife blade pierce her heart.

'I missed you too. But I bet you had a lovely time with all your friends,' she said encouragingly. 'Did you play in the sandpit with Sam?'

Nico stared at her solemnly. 'Can we go home now?'

Kristen set him back on his feet. 'Go and get your coat. We'll stop off at the park, as long as you promise not to climb to the top of the climbing frame.' A shudder ran through her at the memory of how he had fallen and been badly hurt on their last trip to the park. Sometimes she struggled to cope with Nico's exuberance.

As he shot off across the room, she turned to speak to his play-worker, Lizzie. 'How was he today?'

'He's been very withdrawn,' the young woman admitted. 'I tried to persuade him to join in with the activities but it's obvious he's missing his nana.' She gave Kristen a sympathetic look. 'This must be a difficult time for you and Nico. Perhaps, with the summer coming, you could take a holiday. I'm sure it would do you both good.'

There was only one way Kristen could take Nico on holiday, and that was to ask for financial help from his father. Back home at her tiny terraced house, she reread the newspaper article about Sergio's engagement while she was cooking dinner.

It is expected that the couple will celebrate their engagement at a lavish party to be held tonight at the

*Hotel Royale in Bayswater, which was purchased
by the Castellano Group a year ago and has under-
gone a one-hundred-million pound refurbishment.*

If only there was a way she could speak to Sergio before the party. Kristen's heart lurched at the prospect of
revealing to him that he had a son. She glanced into the
living room, expecting to find Nico watching TV, but he
had picked up a framed photograph of Kathleen and was
staring at it with a wistful expression on his face that made
Kristen's heart ache.

'Come and have your dinner,' she said softly.

'I don't want any, Mummy.'

If Nico's appetite didn't pick up soon she would have
to take him back to the doctor, Kristen thought worriedly.
She forced a smile. 'Try and eat a little bit, and then I'll
tell you something exciting.'

She was rewarded with a flicker of interest in Nico's
chocolate button eyes as he ran into the kitchen and took
his place at the table. 'What's ic-citing?'

'Well, I've been thinking that it would be nice if I took
some time off work so that we could have a holiday by the
seaside. Would you like that?'

Nico's wide smile was all the answer she needed. It
brought home to Kristen that she hadn't seen his cheeky
grin for weeks and her heart broke at the thought of her
little boy's sadness. She would make Nico happy again,
she vowed. She would do whatever it took to see him return to his usual sunny nature, and if that meant swallowing her pride and asking his billionaire playboy father for
financial help it would be a small price to pay.

'Honestly, I've no idea why the newspaper printed an article about us being engaged.' Felicity Denholm met Sergio's

frown with a guileless smile. 'I admit I told a journalist that you're in London to finalise a business deal with my father, and I may have mentioned that you're planning to host a party tonight, but that's all I said.'

She perched on the edge of Sergio's desk so that her skirt rode up her thighs and gave a tinkling laugh that grated on his nerves. 'I can't imagine where the story about us planning to get married came from, but you know how the paparazzi like to stretch the truth.'

'In this instance there is not a shred of truth to stretch,' Sergio bit out. His jaw hardened as he struggled to control his impatience. He disliked the media's fascination with his private life and he fiercely resented the publication of a story that was pure fiction.

Felicity shook her glossy chestnut curls over her shoulders. 'Well, we've moved in the same social circles while you have been in London, and we were photographed together the other night when we bumped into one another at the theatre. I suppose it's understandable that the press believe there's something going on between us.' She shifted position so that her skirt rode higher up her thighs and leaned towards Sergio, an artful smile on her red-glossed lips. 'It almost seems a pity to disappoint them, doesn't it?' she murmured.

Sergio's eyes narrowed. Denholm's daughter was an attractive package and he had briefly considered accepting her not very discreet offer to take her to bed. But he had a golden rule never to mix business with pleasure and he had been far more interested in persuading the Earl to sell a property portfolio that included several prime sites in central London than to satisfy his libido with the lovely but, he suspected, utterly self-centred Felicity.

He was sure it had not been purely coincidence that she had appeared at every party he had attended in recent weeks. Her topics of conversation might be limited to fashion and celebrity gossip but she had stalked him with extraordinary determination. It was even possible that Felicity had been following her father's instructions, Sergio mused. The Earl was a wily character who had been forced to sell his property portfolio to pay for the costly upkeep of the family's stately home. Perhaps Charles Denholm had hoped to regain control of his assets by promoting a marriage between his daughter and the Sicilian usurper to his crown.

Sergio was infuriated that he had no way of proving who had planted the engagement story in the paper. All day his temper had simmered while he had dealt with the speculation caused by the article, and the last straw had been a terse telephone conversation with his father, who had demanded to know why he had learned of his son's plan to marry from a newspaper.

'The story is just that—a figment of a journalist's imagination,' he told Tito. 'If I ever decide to marry, you will be the first to know. But don't hold your breath,' he added sardonically.

His father immediately launched into a tirade about it being time Sergio packed in his playboy lifestyle, settled down with a nice Italian girl and, most importantly, produced an heir to continue the Castellano family line.

'You already have an heir in your granddaughter.' Sergio reminded his father of his brother Salvatore's little daughter, Rosa.

'Of course, but she cannot shoulder the responsibility of the company alone,' Tito growled. 'Salvatore is a widower and unlikely to have more children, and so I have to put all my hopes on you, Sergio.'

Sergio was aware of the unspoken message that he was a disappointment to Tito. But he would not pick a bride in the hope of winning the old man's approval. It would be pointless anyway. They both knew he was not the favoured son. And he had no wish to marry. It amazed him that his father did not understand his attitude when Tito's own marriage to Sergio's mother had been a disaster that had ended in bitterness and hatred that had had lifelong consequences for him and his brother.

Dragging his mind from the dark place of his childhood, he jerked to his feet and moved away from the desk where Felicity was still artfully sprawled. He wondered why, despite her obvious charms, he didn't feel a spark of interest in her. In truth, he was becoming bored of meaningless sex. But what other kind of sex was there? he brooded. He had no interest in relationships that demanded his emotional involvement. Work was his driving force, although deep down he acknowledged that his ruthless ambition was partly fuelled by a desire to prove to his father that he was as worthy a son as his twin brother.

In his leisure time, all he required from the women who shared his bed was physical gratification. So why had he been feeling restless lately? What was he searching for when he had everything he could possibly want?

'I have demanded the paper prints an admission that the story is entirely untrue,' he told Felicity. 'I can only apologise for any embarrassment the article may have caused you. As you know, I am giving a party tonight to celebrate the completion of the business deal with your father. Members of the press have been invited, and I intend to make a statement to set the record straight about us.'

Felicity tilted her head and gave him a kittenish smile. 'Or you could ravish me on your desk,' she invited boldly. 'And then, who knows—maybe it won't be necessary for the newspaper to retract the story.'

Maybe he was old-fashioned but he preferred to do the

chasing, Sergio thought as he strode across the room and
held open the door. 'An interesting proposition, but I'm
afraid I must decline,' he drawled.

The young Englishwoman flushed at his rejection and
slid off the desk. 'No wonder you're known as the Ice-
man,' she muttered sulkily. 'Everyone says you have a
frozen heart.'

Sergio gave her a coolly amused smile that did not reach
his eyes. 'Everyone is right. But I have no intention of
discussing my emotions, or lack of them, with you.' He
glanced at his watch and ushered Felicity out of his office.
'And now, if you'll excuse me, I have some work to do.'

The décor of the Hotel Royale was unashamedly opulent.
Clearly the new owners, the Castellano Group, had spared
no expense on the refurbishments and it was easy to see
why the hotel had been awarded five-star status. The clien-
tele were as glamorous as the surroundings, and as Kristen
walked through the marble lobby she was conscious that
her businesslike black skirt and white blouse were definitely not haute couture. It didn't help that her feet were
killing her. She was ruing her decision to wear a pair of
three-inch stilettos that had been an impulse buy and had
sat unworn at the back of her wardrobe for months.

Having made the decision to try and speak to Sergio,
she had arranged for her neighbour to babysit Nico before
she had caught the Tube to Bayswater. She half-expected
the concierge to ask the reason for her visit but the reception area was busy and she walked past the front desk without anyone seeming to notice her. There was a good chance
that Sergio would refuse to see her and so it seemed better to surprise him. The newspaper article had mentioned
that he was staying in his private penthouse suite. As the

lift whisked Kristen smoothly towards the top floor she could feel her heart beating painfully fast beneath her ribs.

It was a crazy idea to have come here, whispered a voice inside her head. Even if she managed to find Sergio, the prospect of telling him he had a son was daunting. She felt sick with nerves and when the lift doors opened she was tempted to remain inside and press the button for the ground floor. Only the memory of Nico's excitement when she had promised to take him on holiday hardened her resolve to ask for financial help from Sergio.

She walked along numerous grey-carpeted corridors with a growing sense of despair that she did not have a clue where his private suite might be. Turning down another corridor, she was confronted with a set of double doors and a sign on the wall announced that she was outside the Princess Elizabeth Function Room.

A waiter emerged from a side door and, catching sight of Kristen, he thrust a tray filled with glasses into her hands. 'Don't just stand there,' he said, sounding harassed. 'They're about to make a toast and some of the guests are still waiting for champagne.'

'Oh, I'm not…' she began to explain, but the waiter wasn't listening as he opened the doors and practically pushed her into the room.

'Hurry up. Mr Castellano is not happy that the party is running late.'

'But…' Kristen's voice trailed off as the waiter hurried away. Glancing around the enormous function room, she realised that her outfit was almost identical to the waitresses' uniform and it was easy to understand how she had been mistaken for a member of staff.

But at least she had found Sergio.

Her heart lurched as her eyes were drawn to the man at the far end of the room. His almost-black hair gleamed like raw silk beneath the blazing lights of the chandeliers. Taller than everyone circled around him and a hundred times more devastatingly handsome than the photo in the newspaper, it was not just his physical attributes that made him stand out from the crowd. Even from a distance, Kristen was conscious of his aura of power and charisma that made all other men seem diminished.

With his stunning looks, huge fortune and blatant virility, Sergio Castellano captured the attention of every woman in the room. But, although he smiled and exuded effortless charm, Kristen sensed a restless air about him. His dark eyes flicked around the room as if he was searching for someone. She caught her breath. He could not possibly know she was here, she reminded herself. And yet in Sicily their awareness of each other had been so acute that they had sensed each other's presence across a crowded room, she remembered.

She watched a woman walk up to him and recognised her as the woman from the paper, Lady Felicity something-or-other. The woman he was planning to marry. The sensation of a knife-blade being thrust between her ribs made Kristen catch her breath. Four years ago Sergio had broken her heart but after all this time she had not anticipated that seeing him again would be so agonising.

He stepped onto a raised platform where a microphone had been set up. Kristen guessed he was about to announce his engagement to Felicity and she was unprepared for the violent feeling of possessiveness that swept through her. For years she had tried to forget Sergio because she had believed he was married to his Sicilian bride. But here he was, about to reveal his plans to marry another woman, while *she* was struggling to bring up his son on her own.

'Ladies and gentlemen—' Sergio's gravelly voice filled the room, and an expectant hush descended over the guests

'—as you are aware, tonight's party is to celebrate the Castellano Group's acquisition of an extensive portfolio of properties from Earl Denholm. Following an article in a certain daily newspaper, there is another matter I would like to address regarding Lady Felicity Denholm and myself…'

'*No! You can't marry her!*'

The words tumbled from Kristen's mouth before she could stop them. Her voice sounded deafeningly loud in the silent room and she felt her face burn as the party guests all turned to look at her. She swallowed as Sergio jerked his head in her direction. Even across the distance of the room, she sensed his shock as he recognised her.

'*Kristen?*'

The husky way he spoke her name, the slight accent on the first syllable, touched something deep inside her. Her eyes locked with his and she felt the same inexplicable connection she had felt the very first time she had seen him. But when they had met on a Sicilian beach Sergio had smiled at her. Now, his shocked expression was rapidly changing to anger—which was hardly surprising when she had just ruined his engagement party, Kristen thought ruefully.

Dear heaven, what had she done? But it was too late to backtrack now.

'It…it isn't right,' she faltered. 'You have responsibilities…you have…' Her nerve failed her. She could not reveal to Sergio that he had a son when he was staring at her with a coldly arrogant expression that froze her blood.

'What are you doing here?' His voice sounded like the crack of a whip and jerked Kristen from her state of stunned immobility. She became aware of the startled faces of the guests around her and felt sick as the magnitude of what she had done hit her. She shouldn't have come and she had to leave, immediately.

She thrust the tray of drinks into the hands of one of the guests and ran across to the double doors just as they opened to allow several waiters bearing trays of canapés to file into the room.

'Stop her!'

The harsh command filled Kristen with panic. A security guard stepped in front of her, blocking her path, and she gave a startled cry as a hand settled heavily on her shoulder and spun her around. She stumbled in her high heeled shoes and fell against Sergio's broad chest.

He stared down at her, his dark eyes blazing with fury. 'What the hell is going on?'

As she stared at his handsome face, the words of apology died on Kristen's lips and her brain stopped functioning. But her senses went into overdrive. The feel of his hand on her shoulder seemed to burn through her thin blouse and the close proximity of their bodies caused her heart to slam against her ribcage. For timeless moments the voices of the guests faded and there was just her and Sergio alone in the universe.

The anger in his eyes turned to curiosity and something else that made the hairs on the back of her neck stand on end. An electrical current seemed to arc between them and Kristen felt heat surge through her body. But then a flashlight flared, half-blinding her, and when Sergio came back into focus his expression was once more furious.

His fingers gripped her shoulder so tightly that she winced. '*Dio*, the press are going to love this,' he said bitterly.

The press! The flashbulbs suddenly made sense. Kristen stared wildly at the flank of photographers who were circling her and Sergio. No doubt the journalists were eager to know why she had interrupted him just as he had been about to announce his engagement. 'Oh, God,' she muttered and, with a strength born of desperation, she tore free from Sergio's hold and shot past the security guard, out into the corridor.

With one of their quarry gone, the journalists crowded around Sergio. 'Mr Castellano, do you want to make a statement?'

'No, I damned well don't,' Sergio growled savagely. What he wanted to do was race after Kristen and find out what she was playing at. He had hardly been able to believe his eyes when he had looked across the ballroom and seen her, and one part of his mind had instantly registered that she was even lovelier than his memory of her.

Enzo, his PR man, appeared beside him and for once the usually unflappable manager looked shaken.

'I think you should say something and explain the situation,' Enzo advised in an undertone meant for Sergio's hearing only. 'Earl Denholm seems to think that you have humiliated his daughter by ending your engagement to her in public, and he's threatening to call off the deal.'

'*Santa Madonna!* There was *no* damned engagement. I assumed Felicity had made that clear to her father.' Sergio's nostrils flared as he struggled to control his temper. He had no wish to talk to the press, but if the deal with Denholm was about to blow up in his face he realised he had no choice.

He spun back round to the journalists, his face now expressionless as he controlled his anger. 'There has been a misunderstanding. Miss Denholm and I are not engaged...'

A microphone was shoved at him. 'Has she called it off because she found out about your mistress?'

'Who is the mystery blonde who just left?'

'Are you planning to marry the waitress?'

Sergio's patience snapped. 'I'm not planning to marry anyone—ever.' He glanced at his PR man. 'Enzo, I'll leave you to deal with this—while I deal with the "mystery blonde",' he said with grim irony, and strode out of the function room.

CHAPTER TWO

WHERE THE HELL was she? Sergio stared up and down the empty corridor before turning left out of the function room. His instincts proved correct as he walked swiftly and turned a corner to see a petite blonde-haired figure at the far end of the passageway.

He was rarely surprised by anything, but tonight he had received a shock that was still causing his heart to thud unevenly. He had seen a ghost from his past, although Kristen Russell—for all her ethereal beauty—was no spectre from the spirit world. She was very real, albeit a woman now rather than the innocent girl he had known four years ago.

An unbidden memory came to him of the first time he had made love to her. It had been a new experience for both of them, he thought wryly. He had been shocked to discover she was a virgin. Before he had met her, and after their relationship had ended, his numerous affairs had been with women whose sexual experience matched his own. It was true that his affair with Kristen had been different from any of his previous relationships, but ultimately it had ended for the same reason his affairs always ended—she had wanted more from him than he could give. When she had left him, he had let her go, knowing there was no point trying to explain his bone-deep mistrust of emotional commitment.

Psychologists would no doubt blame his childhood and in particular his mother as a reason for his inability to connect with women on a deep level. Sergio's mouth curved into a derisive smile. Maybe the shrinks were right. As a child he had taught himself to block out pain—both mental and physical—until nothing could hurt him. It was a trait he had continued as an adult and his freedom from emotional distractions gave him an edge over his business rivals and had earned him a reputation for ruthlessness in the boardroom.

Yet he admitted that he had missed Kristen, and for a while after she had returned to England he had been tempted to follow her and re-ignite the fiery passion that he had never felt so intensely for any other woman. He had resisted because nothing had changed. He could not be the man she wanted. And then there had been Annamaria, and for the only time ever in his life his actions had been driven by love. The cruelty of her untimely death had served as a reminder that even he could not freeze his emotions completely.

Sergio forced his mind from the past and continued his pursuit of Kristen along the corridor which led only to his private suite. She was clearly finding it difficult to keep up a fast pace in her high-heeled shoes and her hips swayed, causing her tightly clad *derrière* to bob tantalisingly in front of his eyes.

His footsteps were muffled by the thick carpet, but Kristen must have sensed someone was behind her because she glanced over her shoulder and gave an audible gasp when she saw him.

'If you're looking for the way out, you won't find it along here,' he told her curtly.

Kristen froze and, realising the futility of continuing along the corridor that appeared to be a dead end, she

slowly turned to face the man who had haunted her dreams
for so long. Sergio had caught up with her and was standing so close that she breathed in the sensual musk of his
cologne. He towered above her, a darkly beautiful fallen
angel in black tailored trousers and matching silk shirt.
Her eyes darted to his face, and she caught her breath as
she felt a kick of sexual awareness in the pit of her stomach. The faint shadow of black stubble on his jaw accentu-
ated his raw masculinity and the curve of his wide mouth
promised heaven. But it was his eyes that trapped her gaze,
as dark and sensuous as molten chocolate, framed by lush
black lashes.

Once, a long time ago, his eyes had held warmth, desire. But now his expression was cold and she sensed his
anger was tightly controlled.

'Besides, it's pointless to look for the exit,' he said in
a dangerously soft voice. 'You won't be going anywhere
until you've explained what in God's name is going on.'

'I'm sorry I interrupted your party,' she said frantically.
'It was a stupid thing to do.' She hesitated, feeling guilty
for the trouble she must have caused. 'I…I hope Miss Denholm isn't too upset.'

He gave a dismissive shrug. 'She is not important.'

Kristen was shocked by his careless dismissal of his
fiancée. 'How can you regard announcing your intention
to marry as unimportant?' She gave him a disgusted look.
'Although it's not the first time you've got engaged so I
suppose it might seem boring.'

Sergio's eyes narrowed at her sarcastic tone. 'What do
you mean?'

Four years of hurt and anger exploded from Kristen.
'You didn't waste much time replacing me in your bed,
did you?' she said bitterly. 'I heard that you'd got engaged

to a Sicilian woman soon after we broke up. That's why I didn't…'

'Didn't what?' he prompted when she broke off abruptly.

'It…it doesn't matter.'

She tore her eyes from his face. The reason she had not contacted him to tell him she was pregnant after she had left Sicily was not only because she had learned of his intention to marry another woman. She had been certain he would not be interested in the child she had conceived by him, and now she questioned why she had considered asking him for financial support for his son.

But surely it was fair that Sergio should take some responsibility for Nico? The voice of reason inside her head refused to be ignored. She had made the decision to ask him for financial help for Nico, and now that they were alone she had the perfect opportunity. Taking a deep breath, she said quickly, 'I was wondering if I could speak to you?'

'Certainly,' he drawled sardonically. 'I'm fascinated to hear why you gatecrashed my party. And after you've explained yourself to me, you can give a statement to the press.

'*Dio!*' His tenuous control over his temper cracked. 'Have you any idea of the furore you've caused? Because of you, my business deal is about to go down the pan.'

So he regarded his engagement to Lady Felicity as a business deal! Kristen shook her head. She had known that Sergio was hard but, even so, she was shocked by the proof of his complete lack of emotion. She must have been mad to think he would agree to give financial assistance for Nico.

'Actually, forget it,' she muttered. 'There's no point in me talking to you.' She tried to walk past him but his hand shot out and gripped her shoulder. Panic sharpened her voice. 'Will you please let me go?'

'You must be joking,' Sergio said grimly. 'Our conversation hasn't even started. Come into my suite so that we can be assured of privacy.'

It was an order rather than an invitation and, before Kristen could argue, he opened the door and steered her into an elegant sitting room. But she barely noticed the décor. The feeling that she had walked into a trap intensified when Sergio closed the door and her vivid imagination pictured her as a fly caught in a spider's web, with no chance of escape.

'Take a seat,' he commanded, waving his hand towards the large sofa in the centre of the room.

Kristen remained standing just inside the door, tension emanating from every pore. Sergio frowned as it occurred to him that she looked nervous. Hell, he had every right to be angry with her, he assured himself as he recalled the scene in the function room. But the possibility that she was afraid of him made him uncomfortable. He raked his hand through his hair. As he stared at her, an image flashed into his mind of her ravaged, tear-stained face at the hospital in Sicily. She had been devastated by what had happened, but soon afterwards she had returned to England and he didn't know if she had coped okay. He should have phoned her to see how she was, his conscience pricked. But at the time it had seemed better to make a clean break, and if he was honest his pride had been hurt by her decision to leave him.

'How are you?' he asked gruffly.

She looked surprised by his softer tone. 'I'm fine... thank you.'

'It's been a long time since we last saw one another.' Irritated with himself for his uncharacteristic lack of savoir faire, Sergio stalked over to the bar. 'Would you like a drink?'

There was a bottle of champagne in an ice bucket and, without waiting for her to reply, he popped the cork, filled two tall flutes and held one out to her. With obvious reluctance, she crossed the room and took the glass from him.

'To old acquaintances, or perhaps I should make that to unexpected visitors,' he said drily. 'Why did you interrupt my party, Kristen?'

Kristen took a gulp of champagne and felt the sensation of bubbles bursting on her tongue. 'I've already told you that I wanted to talk to you…about something important.' She bit her lip, finding it impossible to utter the statement, *By the way, you have a three-year-old child who you've never met.*

Sergio nodded towards the sofa. 'In that case, you had better sit down.'

Sitting seemed the safest option when her legs felt like jelly. Kristen sat, and immediately sank into the soft cushions. She tensed when he sat down next to her and stretched his long legs out in front of him. He extended his arm along the back of the sofa and she couldn't restrain the little quiver that ran down her spine as she imagined his long, tanned fingers stroking her exposed nape where her hair was swept up into a chignon.

An awkward silence fell until he said abruptly, 'So, what did you want to talk to me about?'

Kristen's heart missed a beat and, to steady her nerves, she took another gulp of champagne.

'I…' While she was searching for the right words she made the mistake of looking at him, and whatever she had been about to say died on her tongue when she discovered that he was looking at her in a way that convinced her he was remembering her naked. The bold glitter in his eyes was inappropriate and outrageous, but the damning heat in her breasts as they swelled and strained against her suddenly too-tight bra was even more shocking.

'As you probably know, the Castellano Group owns many hotels around the world,' Sergio was saying. 'Staff issues would normally be dealt with by the Hotel Royale's manager, but I will try to be of help.' He frowned. 'I admit I am puzzled to find you working as a waitress, Kristen. As I recall, you left me to return to university and finish your studies.'

For a few seconds Kristen stared at him blankly, before realisation dawned that he had mistaken her for a waitress. She glanced down at the plain black skirt she had bought to wear to her mother's funeral. As far as Sergio was aware, there was no other reason why she would have been at his private party.

He made the past sound so black and white, she thought bitterly. It was true she had left him to go back to university, but only because he had made it clear that in the long-term there was no place for her in his life. His offer for her to be his temporary mistress had not been enough to persuade her to give up everything she had worked for.

She darted a glance at his hard-boned face. There was no point in raking over the cold embers of their relationship. Everything had been said four years ago. Sergio had wanted her, but only on his terms. As much as she had loved him, she had been angry at his refusal to make compromises and ultimately his intransigence had been proof that he had not cared about her.

Sitting beside Kristen, Sergio inhaled the light floral fragrance of her perfume and he felt a sharp stab of desire. He tried to remind himself of the reason he had brought her to his suite. She owed him an explanation for the fiasco in the function room and he was determined to discover the reason she had interrupted the party. But, as he glanced at her and their eyes met, he was finding it hard to think about anything other than the fact that she was even more desirable than she had been four years ago.

Kristen stiffened when Sergio stretched out his hand and brushed a stray tendril of hair off her cheek.

'You are even more beautiful than I remember.' His deep voice caressed her senses like rough velvet. 'Your eyes are the bright blue of a summer sky and your hair is the colour of ripe corn.'

From any other man the statement would have sounded corny, but Sergio's sexy accent turned the words to poetry. It would be too easy to drown in the molten warmth of his eyes, to fall beneath his spell. Kristen trembled with anger, yet she could not deny the savage, shameful excitement that shot through her. At the party Sergio had been about to announce his engagement to another woman. How dared he now turn his effortless charm on her?

Determined to appear composed, even though she felt anything but, she finished her champagne and hoped he didn't notice her hand was shaking as she placed her glass on the coffee table. 'I should leave,' she said curtly. 'I'm sure Miss Denholm would be devastated if she knew you had invited me into your suite to…to…'

'To what, *cara*?' he drawled. 'You asked to speak to me and I simply agreed to your request.'

'You were flirting with me,' she snapped, stung by the amusement in his voice. 'You had no right to call me beautiful.'

'Why not, when it's the truth?'

Sergio stared at the pulse jerking at the base of Kristen's throat before returning to linger on her mouth, and watched as she moistened her lower lip with the tip of her tongue. The anger he had felt earlier had been replaced with a primitive desire he could not control. She was as tightly wound as a coiled spring and he could almost taste the sexual awareness in the air. Four years was a long time and he had had plenty of other women since Kristen. But none had made his gut twist with raw need like she had done. Like she still did.

His senses were so finely tuned to her that he knew she was going to jump up from the sofa and, before she had time to move, he caught hold of her wrist and forced her to remain seated.

'Let go of me!' She was breathing hard, drawing his eyes to the thrust of her breasts beneath her high-necked blouse. There was something very tantalising about the row of tiny buttons that were fastened right up to her throat. He would never have the patience to unfasten each one, Sergio thought, sexual hunger corkscrewing through him as a memory came into his mind of her small, pale breasts with their rosy tips.

'You are despicable,' Kristen told him hotly. 'You're meant to be hosting a party to celebrate your engagement to a beautiful debutante.'

In truth, Kristen had forgotten about the party, but now guilt joined the gamut of emotions churning inside her. She knew full well that Sergio's emotions were a barren wasteland, but presumably Felicity Denholm was under the illusion that he cared for her. 'That poor woman...'

'I'd save your sympathy if I were you,' Sergio said drily. 'Don't believe everything you read in the gutter press. The engagement story was pure fabrication.'

Kristen swallowed. 'You mean you're not going to marry Lady Felicity?'

'You know my feelings about marriage, *cara*.'

Oh yes, Kristen knew. He had voiced his opinion of marriage loud and clear when they had been together, which had made his decision to marry a Sicilian woman with almost indecent haste after they had broken up all the more hurtful. She closed her eyes against the image in her mind of Sergio and his beautiful dark-haired fiancée. When she had seen the photograph of them in a magazine a few months after she had left Sicily, she had felt sick to her stomach.

Something fluttered against her cheek and she lifted her lashes to find Sergio's face so close to her that she could see the tiny lines fanning around his eyes. The brush of his fingertips across her skin was as soft as gossamer yet she felt as though his touch had branded her.

'What is the real reason you sought my attention to-night?'

Sergio was aware that his voice was not quite steady, but the shock of Kristen's appearance was having a strong effect on him. In the ballroom he had been conscious of a prickling sensation on the back of his neck as he'd been about to address the party guests. He had felt an inexplicable sense of anticipation as he had scanned the room, but he hadn't noticed Kristen until she had spoken.

'First you interrupted the party and then you ran away from me, knowing, I am sure, that I would follow.'

This was the moment to tell him about Nico. Only the words were trapped in her throat, as if some primitive instinct she did not understand warned her to keep her son's existence a secret. It was not a conscious decision. At that moment Kristen was incapable of logical thought. She felt light-headed, and it belatedly occurred to her that she had been too on edge about meeting Sergio to eat any dinner. Drinking a glass of champagne on an empty stomach had been foolish. It must be the effect of the alcohol that was making her heart race, she told herself. The dizzy sensation had nothing to do with the fact that Sergio had lowered his head so that she could feel his warm breath whisper across her lips.

'Was *this* the reason you wanted to see me, *mia bella*?' he demanded.

Her denial died on her lips, or rather it was crushed beneath Sergio's lips as he slanted his mouth over hers and claimed her with the arrogance of a tribal chieftain intent on proving his dominance.

The kiss was hot and hungry, demanding a response from Kristen that, heaven help her, she could not deny, although at first she tried. Her common sense made a last ditch attempt to pull her back from the brink of insanity and gave her the strength of will to clamp her lips together while she tried to push him away. But he was too strong for her to fight him when the ache in her heart was so desperate to be healed.

Sergio traced the determined line of her lips with his tongue, tempting her, teasing her until her lips were no longer firm but soft and pliant. Her breath escaped on a soft gasp as she opened her mouth for him, and he made a gruff sound of pleasure that tugged on her heart. She had never been able to resist him, Kristen acknowledged ruefully. Four years ago she had sensed the loneliness inside him that he took such care to hide and she had responded to it as she did now, with tenderness as well as passion.

Sensing Kristen's capitulation, Sergio gave a growl of triumph. But suddenly they were no longer locked in a battle of wills as the tenor of the kiss subtly altered and became deeper and more intense. The empty years melted away, leaving a scorching desire that had never been doused. When he finally lifted his head, he stared down at her lips—crushed like rose petals after a rain storm— and his eyes glittered.

'For four years you have been in my blood.'

His words sounded almost like an accusation and snapped Kristen back to reality.

'Even while you were married?' she said bitterly. 'If so, then you betrayed your wife as well as me.' A sickening thought struck her. 'Are you still married?'

His expression was unreadable. 'No.'

He offered no explanation of why his first marriage had ended. It was none of her business, Kristen reminded herself. It had been over between her and Sergio a long time ago and it was time to let go of the past. She bitterly regretted coming to his hotel and she had changed her mind about asking him for financial help. Nico was her responsibility.

'You look tired,' he murmured. 'I hope you are not working too hard at the hotel?'

The unexpected softness of Sergio's tone caught Kristen unprepared, and her eyes flew to his face. She flushed when she realised that he still believed she was employed as a waitress at his hotel, but the truth was impossible to explain when she was drowning in his midnight-dark gaze.

She snatched a shallow breath as he lifted his hand and released the clasp that secured her chignon so that her heavy mass of hair uncoiled to midway down her back.

'I'm glad you did not cut it,' Sergio murmured, threading his fingers through the curtain of gold silk.

No way would she admit that she had kept her long hair because he had loved it. It had been easier for Kristen to assure herself that she eschewed having a more complicated style because she could not afford expensive trips to a hair salon.

She tore her eyes from him. 'I should go.' Her composure was balanced on a knife-edge. So why didn't she stand up and walk over to the door? He was still holding her wrist, not tightly, but the rhythmic brush of his thumb pad over her pulse point was seductive, heating her skin, her blood, her desire.

'It's still there, isn't it, *cara*?' His husky voice scraped across her sensitive nerve-endings. 'All it took was one look across a crowded room and the fire burned for both of us.'

It had been the same the very first time he had seen her on the private beach belonging to the Castellano estate, Sergio remembered. He had been furious when he had spotted a trespasser, but when he had caught up with the young woman his anger had died. With her peaches and cream complexion, corn-gold hair and eyes as blue as the sky, she had reminded him of an exquisite doll. But then she had smiled and he had seen that she was a living, breathing, beautiful woman.

She was even more beautiful now, he acknowledged. But the faint purple smudges beneath her eyes gave her a vulnerable air that filled him with irrational anger. If she had remained as his mistress in Sicily he would have ensured that she was financially secure when he had tired of her. Instead she had chosen her independence, but it had not got her far if her cheaply made clothes were anything to go by. She would look stunning in beautifully designed clothes that flattered her slender figure. In his mind he pictured her wearing silk dresses and lace negligees that would glide over her satiny skin as he undressed her.

Why not rekindle the flame? he asked himself. It was not his usual practice to revisit the past. In his experience, by the time an affair ended it was as stale as old toast and nothing could revive his interest. But his interest in Kristen had never completely faded. The sizzling chemistry between them was so hot it was in danger of combusting and proved that there was unfinished business between them.

Kristen was perched on the very edge of the sofa, as

tense and watchful as a nervous gazelle poised to flee. But she had not pulled her wrist from his grasp, and when he glanced at her she swept her long lashes down a fraction too late to hide the hunger in her eyes.

'Tesoro...' he murmured.

'Don't!' The endearment felt like an arrow through Kristen's heart. She jerked to her feet but stumbled on her high heels and fell against Sergio as he leapt up and caught her in his arms. *'Let me go.'* It was a cry from her soul, but he ignored the husky plea and swept her against him, tangling one hand in her hair as he lowered his head and captured her soft, tremulous mouth.

His second kiss was deeper and sweeter than the first, drugging Kristen's senses and breaking through her defences so that she sagged against him while he worked his magic. She could hear her blood thundering in her ears, and when she laid her hands on his chest she could feel his heart beating with the same frantic rhythm as her own. The realisation that she had such a strong effect on him was somehow comforting, and with a low moan she slid her hands to his shoulders and kissed him with all the wild passion that had been locked inside her since they had parted.

This was madness. Kristen's mind whirled as the walls of the room spun when Sergio lifted her into his arms. She knew she should stop him, especially when she opened her eyes and discovered that he had carried her into his bedroom. The sight of a vast bed draped with a black satin bedspread should have rung alarm bells in her head. But when he sank down onto the mattress, still cradling her in his arms, and sought her mouth once more, it seemed so right and so natural to part her lips and allow his tongue to probe between them in an erotic exploration that stole her breath.

How many nights had she dreamed of Sergio making

love to her? Kristen wasn't sure if this was really happening. It seemed impossible that her most intimate fantasies were coming true, but as his mouth plundered her lips, demanding her ever more passionate response, everything faded and there was just this man and this moment in time when the universe stopped.

CHAPTER THREE

'LA MIA BELLA Kristen!' Sergio murmured huskily.

The unexpected tenderness in his voice drove the lingering doubts from Kristen's mind. He had called her his beautiful Kristen and the fire in his eyes, the hard glitter of sexual need that he made no attempt to hide, made her feel beautiful. Caught up in a dream world, he was the only reality and she clung to him, curling her arms around his neck to prevent him from lifting his mouth from hers. His dark hair felt like silk as she shaped his skull with her fingertips, and when she moved her hand to his jaw the faint shadow of growth felt abrasive against her palm.

His hands were equally busy tracing restlessly over her arms, shoulders, the length of her spine, as if he was reacquainting himself with her body by touch. When he stroked his fingertips lightly across her breasts the sensation was so intense that she could not hold back a soft cry of pleasure. It had been so long since she had felt the sweet stirring of sexual desire but now it coursed through her veins, heating her blood so that her cheeks grew flushed and she felt boneless and utterly wanton.

Somehow, without realising that they had moved, Kristen found herself lying flat on her back and Sergio was tugging at the buttons on her blouse.

He cursed. 'The patience of a saint is required to undo

these damned things. And I have never professed to piety,'
he growled as he gripped the hem of her blouse and pushed
it up to her neck.

Her bra was made of sheer, stretchy material that offered no resistance when Sergio tugged the cups down to
expose her naked breasts. As far as Kristen was concerned
her small breasts had never been her best feature, but his
breath hissed between his teeth as he stared down at her.
'Your body is *perfetto*,' he said thickly. He touched her
nipples delicately, almost reverently, creating starbursts
of pleasure that grew stronger as he rolled the tight nubs
between his fingers until they were as hard as pebbles.

A fiery path shot down Kristen's body and unerringly
found the heart of her femininity. She felt the moistness
between her legs and squeezed her thighs together to try to
ease the ache of need that throbbed insistently there. Her
nipples felt hot and swollen from Sergio's ministrations,
and when he replaced his fingers with his mouth and laved
each rosy peak with his tongue she gasped in delight at
the magic he was creating, and felt herself sinking deeper
into a swirling black vortex of pleasure.

He kissed her mouth again, a hard, fierce kiss that lacked
his earlier tenderness as raw, primitive need took over and
set its own urgent demands. Kristen recognised Sergio's
hunger and shared it. He was her man, her master, and
her body was impatient to feel him inside her. Her fingers
scrabbled with his shirt buttons and a tremor ran through
her when she parted the silk and skimmed her hands over
his naked torso, revelling in the feel of his satiny skin that
gleamed olive-gold in the lamplight.

His chest was covered in whorls of dark hair that arrowed over his flat abdomen and disappeared beneath the
waistband of his trousers. She trailed her fingertips down
his body and caught her breath when she felt the swollen

length of his arousal. A memory of his powerful manhood driving into her was almost enough to make her come before he had even touched her intimately, and he must have sensed her desperation for he groaned something in a harsh tone as he caught hold of the hem of her skirt and shoved it up to her waist.

Kristen wished she was wearing prettier underwear rather than a pair of plain white briefs and nude-coloured tights that were surely a passion-killer. But of course she hadn't dressed for her meeting with Sergio with seduction in mind. Reality made an unwelcome reappearance into her dream world, and she froze. *Was she mad?* For the past four years she had schooled herself to believe that she was over Sergio and he meant nothing to her, but within an hour of meeting him again she was lying half-naked on his bed and he was about to…

What he was about to do became very clear as he knelt above her and undid his zip. Kristen's heart lodged in her throat as she watched him drag his trousers and boxers down his thighs to reveal his massive erection. His body was magnificent, a powerhouse of muscle and sinew that at this moment was primed to give and receive sexual pleasure.

Apprehension and doubt faded as she sank back into her dream world. Reality had no place here tonight. This was one stolen night of pleasure to repay her for all the lonely nights when she had huddled in bed, dry-eyed because the ache inside her went too deep for tears. Sergio's desire for her, the proof of which was jabbing impatiently between her legs, made her feel like the carefree girl she had been when she had met him. Making love with him then had been uncomplicated—passion in its purest form—without the baggage of hopes and expectations that had come later.

'*Cara*, it has to be now,' Sergio groaned. Dull colour

seared along his razor-edge cheekbones. 'You unman me,' he said harshly. 'You are the only woman to ever make me lose control.'

Good, Kristen wanted to tell him. You are the only man, full stop. She did not want to think of him having sex with other women. It was easier not to think at all, just to feel, to touch and taste him and absorb the essence of his raw masculinity. When he peeled her tights and knickers down she lifted her hips to aid him and opened her legs as he stroked his finger over her opening before slipping it into her slick warmth. She was on fire instantly and gave a little moan as he moved his hand rhythmically and brought her swiftly to the brink.

'Sergio…' She whispered his name like a prayer, a plea, unable to deny her need. She wondered why he hesitated until she saw him slide a condom over his arousal, and then he moved over her and pushed her legs wider apart as he positioned himself and eased slowly forward so that the tip of his shaft pushed into her silken folds.

The sensation of him possessing her inch by incredible inch, and pausing to allow her unused muscles to stretch and accommodate him, was almost too good to bear. Kristen's heart was pounding, not only with the pleasure he was inducing but with a fierce joy that went beyond the physical experience of making love with him. Her breath left her on a soft sigh that brought a smile to Sergio's lips.

'Do you like that, *cara*?' He thrust deeply and gave an unsteady laugh when she gasped. 'The best is yet to come, *mia belleza*.'

And so he proved as he slid his hands beneath her bottom and established a fast rhythm that drove her wild as each powerful thrust of his body took her inexorably higher towards the peak. She clung to him, digging her fingertips into his shoulders as the ride became faster and more urgent. Caught up in the maelstrom, her body moving in perfect accord with Sergio's, Kristen lost the sense of them being two individual people, for they had become one unity, one body, one soul.

What was it about this woman that made having sex with her such an intensely sensual experience? Sergio wondered. He had had many mistresses, but only Kristen had ever answered a need deep inside him that he could not explain or define. One thing he did know was that she tested his self-control to its limits. This was not going to be his finest performance, he acknowledged ruefully. He could already feel the pressure building inside him, and he could hear his blood thundering in his ears as he fought against the tide of pleasure that threatened to drag him under.

He wanted it to be good for her. And somehow concentrating on her pleasure lessened the urgency of his own desire so that he was able to pace his strokes and maintain a steady rhythm of hard thrusts deep into her. Her breathless moans told him her orgasm was close and he clenched his jaw as he felt the first spasms rack her body. Suddenly she tensed and arched her hips and the soft cry she gave decimated his restraint. She was so beautiful with her rose-flushed face and her gold hair spread like a halo across the pillows. For a few seconds he glimpsed an unguarded expression in her eyes that shook him, but before he could question what he had seen her lashes drifted down as her body trembled in the throes of a shattering climax.

His own release was almost instantaneous and the power of his orgasm stunned him. His body shook as his seed pumped from him and his lungs burned as he dragged in oxygen. His limbs felt heavy as a delicious lassitude swept through him. Sergio could not remember ever feeling so relaxed. Kristen felt so warm and soft beneath him and he was reluctant to break the spell that held him captive.

The strident ringtone of his phone was a violent intrusion that shattered the peace. With a curse Sergio reached for his phone on the bedside table, intending to cut the call, but he frowned when he glanced at the caller display and saw that his brother was on the line. A call from home was unexpected and he could not ignore it.

'Excuse me, *cara*. I have to take this,' he murmured as with one hand he hauled his trousers back up and climbed off the bed.

Kristen watched Sergio walk out of the room, and only when he had closed the door behind him did she release her breath on a shuddering groan. The sleepy contentment that had swept through her in the aftermath of making love with him had disappeared and her limbs trembled uncontrollably as reaction set in.

Sickening shame churned in her stomach. She must have been out of her mind, she thought grimly. There was no excuse for her behaviour and no use blaming one glass of champagne for her loss of inhibition. The unpalatable truth was that she had been swept away on a tide of lust. But now she felt like a cheap tart and she couldn't blame Sergio if he thought she was an easy lay. Her humiliation was compounded when she glanced down at her dishevelled clothes. Her skirt was bunched up around her waist to reveal her naked thighs.

Sitting up, she tugged her bra back into place and pulled her blouse down. Her breasts felt tender and when she slid off the bed the slight soreness between her legs was another cringing reminder of her stupidity. Her knickers and tights were lying on the carpet where Sergio had dropped them. Their passion had been so intense that he had not even taken the time to undress himself or her, and the sight of her discarded underwear emphasised how grubby the whole unedifying event now seemed.

Glancing at her watch, she was shocked to find that only an hour had passed since she had run away from the party. When Sergio had taken her to bed she had lost all sense of time, but the reality was that they had had a quickie, and now, in a situation that was painfully familiar, he had abandoned her and was on his phone, no doubt discussing business.

Sergio's insistence on putting work before everything else, including their relationship, had come between them four years ago and was one reason why Kristen had walked away from him. Nothing had changed, she thought, choking back a bitter laugh that was dangerously close to a sob. Did he expect her to simply lie here and wait for him to come back to the bedroom? If so, then he was going to be disappointed.

Her shoes were at the end of the bed where she had kicked them off. She hurriedly pulled on her knickers but shoved her tights into her handbag, not wanting to waste a second putting them on. To her huge relief, the sitting room was empty and Sergio's voice came from another room which she guessed was a study. She glimpsed him through the half-open door, but he had his back to her and didn't turn his head as she walked noiselessly across the thick carpet and let herself out of the suite.

'I can't say how much longer I'll be staying in London. I'm not certain of my plans,' Sergio told his brother, aware as he spoke that his meticulously organised schedule had just altered radically. 'I'm sorry to hear that Tito is unwell, but it sounds like the situation is under control.'

'This latest lung infection is an indication that age is catching up with Papà, and he is becoming frailer. But he is responding to the antibiotics and there is no need for you to rush back. Whoever this woman is, she must be quite something for you to have interrupted your schedule for her,' Salvatore commented drily.

The image of Kristen spread half-naked across his bed slid into Sergio's mind and he felt a tightening in his groin. But he had no intention of confiding to Salvatore that he'd just had the best sex of his life. 'What makes you think it's a woman?'

A sardonic laugh sounded down the phone. 'With you it's always a woman, Sergio.'

He would be the first to admit that he was no angel, Sergio acknowledged as he ended the call. He had a high sex drive and a low boredom threshold. Only one woman had warmed the coldness inside him but he was pretty sure that the reason Kristen had lingered in his mind for the past four years was because he had never found the same intense sexual compatibility with anyone else. Having sex with her again had proved that theory. *Dio*, he had been so hot for her that he had behaved like a rutting bull tonight, he thought grimly. There had been no finesse in the way he had made love to her, but next time he would take things slower and satisfy all her needs as well as his own.

He was not unduly surprised to find the bedroom was empty when he strolled in. He assumed that Kristen was in the bathroom, but when she did not reappear after five minutes and there were no sounds to indicate she was running a shower or bath he tried the door and discovered it was unlocked.

Where the hell was she? His stomach gave a sickening lurch of disappointment as it became clear that she had gone. His earlier good mood gave way to frustration. He couldn't understand why she would take off without a word. Sergio raked his hand through his hair and dismissed an uncharacteristic flash of self-doubt. The sex had been as good for her as it had for him, of that he was certain. Just thinking about the little moans of pleasure she had made when she had come was having a predictable effect on his body.

But maybe, inconceivable though it was to him, she was shy and felt embarrassed that they had fallen into bed within minutes of seeing each other again. It hadn't been something he had planned when he had invited her into his hotel suite, Sergio thought ruefully. But it wasn't surprising when their passion for each other four years ago had been as scorching as a Sicilian summer. Now that Kristen had reappeared in his life he did not intend to let her go until his desire for her was utterly sated. And fortunately he would easily be able to find her. She was an employee at the hotel and her details would be on file.

Reassured that she could not slip away from him, he poured himself another glass of champagne and put a call through to the Hotel Royale's manager requesting information on a waitress named Kristen Russell. Half an hour later, when it became clear that there had never been a woman of that name employed at the hotel, his ice-cold anger made the hapless manager more nervous than if he had given vent to his temper. And, after he had dismissed the man and was alone again, Sergio stared out at the London night sky with eyes that were hard and empty of emotion.

Monday morning brought rain and grey skies that ended the previous week's promise that summer was on the way. The postman delivered a pile of bills which Kristen opened while she simultaneously ate a piece of toast, loaded the washing machine and packed Nico's lunch box.

'Do you want to take an apple or a banana to nursery?'

She sighed when he made no response. 'Please choose, sweetheart. We must get going or I'll be late for work.'

'Don't want to go to nursery.' Nico's bottom lip trembled ominously. 'We can stay home today, Mummy.'

Kristen glanced at the clock and took a deep breath, determined to remain patient. It didn't help matters that she was tired and the house was a mess after Steph and a few other friends had come over on Sunday evening and stayed until late. Steph had needed cheering up after she'd received her decree absolute, and had brought several bottles of wine with her—which had all been drunk.

She would have to take a trip to the bottle bank after work, Kristen thought ruefully. At least trying to help her friend had kept her mind from dwelling on what had happened when she had met Sergio on Friday evening. But memories of making love with him had kept her awake for most of last night and consequently she had a thumping headache.

'Today is a work day for me and a nursery day for you,' she explained gently to Nico. 'You'd better put your Wellingtons on as it's raining.'

It took another five minutes to persuade Nico into his coat and locate keys, her handbag and his backpack. The rain was falling harder, bouncing off the pavement and drumming loudly onto her umbrella as she clasped Nico's hand and tried to hurry him along the street, but they had only gone a few paces when he stopped dead.

'I don't want to go.' Two fat tears slid down Nico's cheeks and as Kristen looked at his unhappy face she felt a clenching pain deep in her stomach that reminded her of the contractions she had felt when she had given birth to him. More than anything in the world she wished she could spend the day with him, but she couldn't rely on a fairy godmother to pay the gas bill and the council tax demand.

'Sweetheart, you know you have to go to nursery while I'm at work. I've got an early appointment and I can't be late.'

Out of the corner of her eye Kristen caught sight of a sleek black saloon car driving past. It was noticeable because of the slow speed it was travelling and, for some inexplicable reason, she felt a tiny flicker of unease when she realised that the car's heavily tinted windows hid the occupants from view. Her sense of trepidation increased as the car pulled into a parking space a little further up the road. Stop being paranoid, she ordered herself angrily. After her desperate flight from the Hotel Royale on Friday night her nerves had been on edge all weekend, but her fear that Sergio would find her had faded when she had reminded herself that he had no idea where she lived.

She was jerked from her thoughts as Nico tugged his hand free and ran back up the street. 'Hey…where are you going?' Kristen hurried after him and caught hold of him as he reached the garden gate.

'I don't want to go to nursery,' he said mutinously.

Sensing a tantrum brewing, Kristen knew she had to regain control. 'Well, I'm sorry but you are going,' she told him firmly.

Nico began to cry loudly, his chest heaving with the force of his sobs, and as Kristen stood in the pouring rain, knowing that she was going to miss her train and would have to reschedule all her morning's appointments, she felt like howling too. 'That's enough, Nico.' Her voice sounded sharper than she had intended and guilt swamped her when he wept harder.

'Kristen, what the hell is going on?'

Dear heaven! Her heart slammed against her ribs. She had believed she was safe, felt sure that she would never see

Sergio again. But against the odds he had found her. Squaring her shoulders, she spun round to face her nemesis.

'Why did you run away the other night?'

She could almost believe he sounded hurt, but she must have imagined it, Kristen told herself. She, better than anyone, knew that Sergio did not waste his time and energy on emotions. She tore her eyes from his, shaken and confused by the intensity of his gaze. It did not help her equilibrium that he looked gorgeous in a pale grey suit and navy silk shirt. Dark patches were forming on his jacket as he stood in the rain, and his hair was already soaked and fell forwards onto his brow.

'How did you find me?'

His eyes narrowed at her cool tone and he raked a hand impatiently through his wet hair.

'With considerable difficulty,' he said tersely. 'You lied to me, Kristen. You don't work at the hotel.'

'I never said I did. You just jumped to the conclusion that I was an employee.' She flushed at his derisive look. Despite the protection of the umbrella, her long braided hair was damp and stray tendrils were stuck to her face. She shot Sergio a glance and quickly looked away again, hating her body's involuntary response to him. 'Look, I can't stop. I'm late.'

'You can't stop! *Dio*, I haven't come here for a chat!' he exploded, and Kristen suddenly realised that beneath his icy control he was furious. 'I take it you haven't seen this morning's headlines?'

She gave him a puzzled look. 'No, I haven't. Why?'

Instead of replying, he unbuttoned his jacket, pulled out a newspaper and thrust it at her. The headline, in bold print, seemed to leap off the page.

Billionaire Dumps Debutante for Domestic!

Kristen stared in horror at the photograph beneath the

headline, which showed her leaning against Sergio, cling-ing to his shirt front and staring up at him like a love-sick idiot.

'What on earth…?' The picture had been taken when Sergio had chased after her to stop her fleeing from his party, she realised. She had stumbled on her stupid high heels and grabbed hold of him for support. Frantically she skimmed the newspaper article.

Sicilian love-rat Sergio Castellano has certainly lived up to his reputation as a serial playboy. Feath-ers flew when his fiancée and mistress both turned up at a party at the Hotel Royale. Felicity Denholm was said to be distraught when Sergio left the party to chase after the mystery blonde who is believed to be a waitress at the hotel.

'Oh, heavens,' she said faintly.

'Is that all you can say?' he demanded savagely. 'Thanks to your little escapade on Friday evening, my business deal with Earl Denholm is threatened, my personal reputation is on the line and the price of the Castellano Group's shares has plummeted.'

Kristen bit her lip. 'I'm sorry. I don't know what else to say.'

'My PR manager is frantically putting a damage lim-itation plan into action and has written a statement for you to make to journalists.' Sergio glanced at his watch. 'I've arranged a press conference for nine o'clock. If we go now we should make it on time. My car is over there.' He swung round and took a few steps but, realising that Kristen was not following him, he glanced back at her, impatience etched onto his hard features. 'Come along. What are you waiting for?'

'I can't go with you. I have to take Nic…' She broke off and watched tensely as Sergio walked back to her. He seemed to realise for the first time that she wasn't alone and glanced over her shoulder to the child standing behind her. Kristen was thankful that Nico's baseball cap hid his face but, as Sergio continued to stare, she gripped her son's hand.

'Is he your child?' There was a curious note in his voice she could not define.

Kristen swallowed. 'Yes.' She tried to step past Sergio and her tension escalated when he did not move out of her way. 'Please excuse us. I need to get him to nursery.'

'So are you married? You have a different surname, which is one reason why it took me forty-eight hours to find you,' he revealed with an edge of impatience. 'I was searching for Kristen Russell, but your name now is Lloyd. Is that the name of your child's father?'

Nico had been standing silently, his gaze fixed curiously on the stranger. But, perhaps conscious of Sergio's scrutiny, he suddenly pulled off his cap and held it out to him. 'My hat's got Bertie Bear on it—see?' he said innocently.

The ensuing silence only lasted for a few seconds, but to Kristen it seemed as though time was suspended and it was a lifetime before Sergio reacted.

'*Santa Madonna!*' His breath hissed between his teeth and he jerked his head back as if he had been slapped. He flicked his eyes to Kristen's white face and then back to the child by her side. 'It's not possible,' he said hoarsely. 'You lost the baby. I was with you at the hospital when you had the miscarriage.'

CHAPTER FOUR

KRISTEN DID NOT reply—could not, when there was no oxygen in her lungs—but she held Nico's hand tighter as Sergio crouched down so that he could study the little boy's face.

'*He is my son.*'

It was a statement, not a question, and there was a note of awed wonder in his voice that made Kristen's stomach clench. She had felt the same sense of amazement when she had looked at her son for the first time minutes after she had given birth to him. But she was startled by the raw emotion when Sergio spoke. She did not understand his reaction. It had been obvious when she had suffered the miscarriage that he had not shared her devastation, and in fact had been relieved that she was no longer carrying his child.

There was no point in denying the truth, yet Kristen hesitated. Three days ago she had made the decision to tell Sergio he had a child, so why did she now feel such trepidation and an urge to snatch Nico into her arms? She forced her throat to work and whispered, 'Yes, he's yours.'

Sergio straightened up and growled something ugly in a low tone meant for Kristen's ears only. 'I don't understand. You were bleeding when I rushed you to the hospital.'

His words brought back painful memories of that terrible day. She had felt so scared, Kristen remembered. She had not known she was pregnant until a doctor at the hospital explained that she had lost the baby, but she had been overwhelmed with sadness and guilt that perhaps the miscarriage had somehow been her fault.

She bit her lip. 'When I had the miscarriage I lost Nico's twin. But at the time I was unaware that I was carrying two babies,' she explained shakily. 'I only found out I was still pregnant after I returned to England.'

'But you didn't think to tell me?' Sergio's expression was coldly contemptuous. His barely controlled anger sparked Kristen's temper and helped to lessen the feeling of guilt churning inside her.

'I did think of letting you know but, before I could contact you, I saw the announcement of your engagement to a woman in Sicily. I read about your engagement in a magazine at my doctor's surgery, but the magazine was a few weeks out of date,' she explained shakily. 'By the time I read the article I realised that you must already be married and…and I guessed you would not welcome the news that I was expecting your illegitimate child.'

Sergio's jaw clenched. His skin was drawn so tight over the bones of his face that his cheekbones were sharply prominent.

'*He is my child,*' he said hoarsely. 'What right did you have to keep him a secret from me?'

'*You had married someone else!*'

Kristen felt Nico give a start at the sound of her raised voice and she silently cursed herself. She gave him a reassuring smile and replaced his cap on his head to protect him from the rain.

'I can't talk now,' she muttered to Sergio. 'Nico is getting soaked, and I don't want him to spend all day at nursery school in damp clothes.'

Nico's bottom lip trembled. 'Mummy, I don't want to go.'

Somehow she managed to keep her voice calm. 'Sweetheart, we've been through this and I've explained that you have to go today.' Her heart sank when Nico started to cry again, and she tensed when Sergio stepped closer to prevent her from walking away from him.

'Surely he's too young to go to school? He can only be a couple of months over three years old.'

'He was three in March. He doesn't go to school yet, but he attends a day-care nursery.'

'Which he clearly doesn't enjoy,' Sergio said tautly. 'Does he cry like this every day?'

Kristen stiffened at the note of censure in his voice. 'He loves it once he's there,' she said defensively. 'It's just the thought of going that upsets him.'

'Then why send him?'

'Because I have to work.' She lifted her chin and met Sergio's unreadable gaze, her own faintly challenging. 'Bringing up a child is expensive.'

'If I had known you were pregnant, naturally I would have supported you and my son.'

'How would you have done? Would you have told your wife about your illegitimate child?'

Kristen could not hide the bitterness in her voice. They were going round and round in circles, she thought wearily. 'This is a pointless conversation. In case you hadn't noticed, you're soaked to the skin.' She tore her eyes from the front of his shirt, which was now so wet that she could clearly see the delineation of his six-pack beneath the navy silk. 'I'm late for work, and Nico should be at nursery, so please move out of the way and allow us to pass.'

Sergio's cold eyes flashed with sudden fire as his hand shot out and fastened like a band of steel around her wrist.

'Don't you dare dismiss me,' he said savagely. 'This conversation is far from over.'

He glanced at Nico and must have realised that his aggression was scaring the little boy for he said in a softer voice, 'I'll drive you to his nursery and then to your workplace. Where do you work, anyway? Your name wasn't on the list of staff at the Hotel Royale, so why were you working as a waitress there the other night?'

Kristen flushed. 'It was a misunderstanding. I'm not a waitress…I'm a physiotherapist.'

His eyes narrowed. 'Then what were you doing at my party?'

'Can we talk about it another time?' she said desperately. Now was not the moment to admit that she had intended to ask him for a financial contribution for Nico.

'You can be sure we will talk later,' Sergio promised grimly. He turned his head from her as if the sight of her disgusted him and crouched down in front of Nico once more.

'Hello, Nico.' A faint tremor shook his voice and his expression softened as he studied the little boy. 'Would you like to have a ride in my car?'

Kristen bit her lip. The man she had known four years ago had been so adept at hiding his feelings that she had believed him to be emotionless, but Sergio was clearly struggling for self-control.

Nico was sufficiently intrigued to cease crying. 'What's your car?'

'It's that big black one just along the road.'

'I don't have a child seat for him,' Kristen muttered.

'I believe there is an integrated booster seat in the rear of the car.' Sergio dismissed her objection without sparing her a glance and focused his attention on his son.

'What do you say, Nico? Will you stop crying if I take

you to your nursery school in my car? *Bene,*' he murmured when the little boy nodded. 'Come on then, let's get out of this rain, shall we?'

Kristen could not define the feeling that swept through her as she watched her son trustingly put his small hand into Sergio's larger one. Nico was usually shy with people he didn't know and the only male contact he'd had in his life was with elderly Mr Parker who lived next door. Yet he was happily walking off with Sergio and seemed to have forgotten about *her*, Kristen thought with a pang.

'You shouldn't encourage him to go off with a stranger,' she said sharply as she walked quickly along the pavement to the waiting car. 'He doesn't know you. I don't want him to think it is okay to get into a stranger's car.'

Sergio's eyes glittered. 'It is not my fault he doesn't know me. But that unfortunate situation will not continue and he will soon know me very well.'

Something in his tone caused a hard knot of dread to settle in Kristen's chest. 'What do you mean?'

'I mean that I want to be involved in my son's life. *Dio,*' he growled when she made a choked sound, 'I have just discovered that I am his father. Did you expect me to simply walk away from him? Boys need their fathers,' he added in a curiously driven voice.

'At his age, Nico needs his mother more than anyone else,' Kristen said desperately.

'A mother who dumps him in a nursery all day.' Sergio's tone was scathing. 'A three-year-old child requires more parental attention than you are giving him.'

Kristen reeled as if he had physically struck her. 'Nico is my world and I would willingly give my life for him. How dare you say that I don't give him enough attention?' Her voice trembled with anger at the accusation. Yet it was true that only three days ago she had decided she needed to spend more time with her little boy to help him get over the death of his grandmother, her conscience reminded her.

Nico's voice dragged her from her thoughts. Sergio's driver had lifted him onto the booster seat in the back of the car and secured the seat belt around him, but now there was a tiny quiver of uncertainty in Nico's voice as he said, 'Are you coming, Mummy?'

'Of course I'm coming with you.' Tearing her eyes from Sergio's impenetrable gaze, Kristen handed his driver her umbrella and climbed into the car. To her dismay, Sergio slid in next to her instead of walking round to the other passenger door. His wet clothes were moulded to his body and Kristen could feel his hard thighs pressed against her through his rain-soaked trousers. He smelled of rain and expensive cologne, and the combination was so intensely sensual that her heart-rate quickened.

Heat pooled low in her pelvis and she instinctively lifted her hand to her throat to hide the urgent thud of her pulse just as Sergio turned his head towards her. His brows lifted mockingly and she flushed, aware that he had understood the reason for her betraying gesture. She had never been able to disguise her fierce awareness of him, she acknowledged bleakly.

Four years ago she had fallen for him so hard that nothing else had seemed important, not even her gymnastics training and the goal of winning a world championship title that had been her dream since childhood. When she had met Sergio she had dreamed instead of marriage, children, the whole happy-ever-after scenario. But the dream had ended when she had lost their child.

'Perhaps it is for the best.' Even now the memory of Sergio's words had the power to hurt her. After she had lost their baby, she had been distraught. But he had paced around the hospital room and avoided making eye contact

with her. His words had ripped her emotions to shreds as much as the agonising stomach cramps that had torn through her body during the miscarriage. The knowledge that he had not wanted their child had made her realise what a fool she had been to believe in fairy tales.

While Kristen gave the driver directions to the nursery, Sergio leaned his head against the back of the seat, conscious that his wet clothes were sticking to the car's leather upholstery. But he did not give a damn that he could wring the water from his bespoke silk shirt or that his hand-stitched leather shoes made by the finest Italian craftsmen were probably ruined. Everything else faded to insignificance compared to the discovery that he had a son.

He looked over at Nico and felt a curious sensation as if his heart was being squeezed in a vice. His child—his little boy! It still hadn't completely sunk in that the angelic-looking *bambino* was his flesh and blood. But the evidence spoke for itself. Nico bore all the markings of his Sicilian ancestry with his almost-black hair that, unlike Sergio's own cropped style, was a mass of baby curls and his dark brown eyes. His complexion was olive-toned, although he was worryingly pale, which was not surprising when he had spent the first three years of his life in England's unpredictable climate, Sergio thought bitterly. He was sure the child would thrive in Sicily's warm sunshine, and the sooner he could take him home to the Castellano estate the better.

Nico…he silently sounded his son's name. He was glad Kristen had given him an Italian name but it was a small consolation when she had stolen the first precious years of the little boy's life from him. Anger burned like a branding-iron in his gut as his eyes were drawn to the woman sitting stiffly beside him. How could someone so goddamn beautiful be such a treacherous bitch?

He swallowed the bile that had risen in his throat. Three nights ago he had decided that he wanted her back in his life. Now he wanted… Slowly he unfurled his clenched fist and sought to control his rage. He knew what he was capable of if he lost his temper—and so did his mother's lover who, when Sergio had been fifteen, had made the mistake of hitting him.

Dio! It had been twenty years ago, but the memory was still vivid in his mind and the shame he felt at what he had done still scourged his soul. It was no excuse that, after years of suffering physical abuse from his unpredictable, alcoholic mother, he had snapped, no excuse that for the first time in his life he had been driven to defend himself and hit back.

It had taken two security guards who had worked at the apartment block where his mother lived to pull him off her lover, while she had screamed hysterically. She had accused him of being a savage, he remembered grimly. After everything she had put him through—the misery of his childhood and the cruelty he had suffered almost daily— the irony had not been lost on him. The punk she had been sleeping with had deserved every blow Sergio had inflicted on him, but afterwards he had felt ashamed that he had sunk so low. He hated to admit that for a few seconds he had felt empowered by fighting back, and shockingly there had been a moment when he had imagined it was his mother he was hitting rather than her lover.

He had felt sickened with self-disgust. He wasn't an animal, and he had vowed that day never to lose his temper again. He was almost afraid of his physical strength, afraid of what he was capable of. His anger had to be controlled, and the only way to do that was to cut off all his emotions. And so he had taught himself to bury his feelings and use his brain rather than his fists. Don't get mad, get even, was his rule in life.

He stared unseeingly out of the car window, his mind locked in the past. A memory slid into his mind of watching Patti—his mother had insisted that he use her name instead of calling her Mamma—opening a letter and reacting furiously when she learned that she had been turned down for a film role. His heart had sunk when she had reached for the gin bottle, knowing that her drinking would be a prelude to violence. Sure enough, she had punished him for some misdemeanour; he couldn't remember what he was supposed to have done to warrant the sting of the cane across the backs of his legs.

He had been six years old, a lonely little boy in New York, desperately missing his home in Sicily and unable to understand why Papa did not come for him. His mother had told him it was because Papa did not love him.

Sergio dragged his mind back to the present. He sensed Kristen's tension and the realisation that she was nervous of him left a bitter taste in his mouth. He would never lay a finger on her in anger. The idea was abhorrent to him. But he hated her for what she had done, and he hated even more the swift, hot surge of desire that arrowed through him as he stared at her delicate features.

'How long does Nico stay at nursery every day?' he asked abruptly.

'He stays there all day while I'm at work. I usually drop him off at eight-thirty and collect him at five-thirty.'

'Aren't you concerned that being away from you for so long could be detrimental for him?'

'I admit it's not a perfect situation,' Kristen replied sharply, bristling at the criticism in his voice, 'but I have no choice. I have a career...'

'Ah, yes…your career.'

She frowned. 'Why did you say it in such a sneering tone? Yes, I have a career. I studied hard at university to qualify as a physiotherapist, and I'm proud of what I've achieved. I have no choice but to work…'

'You had a choice,' Sergio said harshly. 'You could have told me about my son when he was born and I would have made sure that you did not have to dump him in day-care while you pursued your precious career.'

Kristen was prevented from replying as the car pulled up outside the nursery building and Sergio immediately stepped out onto the pavement. But inwardly she was seething at the way he had made her out to be an uncaring mother. The only reason she worked long hours was to keep a roof over their heads and she missed Nico desperately while she was away from him. She unfastened the little boy's seat belt and lifted him out of the car, but when she tried to set him on his feet he clung tightly to her.

'Mummy, I want to stay with you.'

Nico's play-worker had advised that it was best to ignore his tears and say goodbye quickly and cheerfully. 'The minute you've gone he's no longer upset, and he's quite happy to play with his friends,' Lizzie had assured her. With that in mind, Kristen prised his arms from around her neck and walked him briskly into the nursery. She was conscious of Sergio following close behind her but she did her best to ignore his unsettling presence.

The play-worker met them in the hallway. 'Hello, Nico, have you come to have fun with us today?' Lizzie said brightly.

Kristen saw the curious look she gave Sergio and realised she would have to introduce him. 'Why don't you go and find Sam?' she asked Nico. She waited until he had gone into the play-room and then turned to Lizzie.

'This is Sergio Castellano…' she hesitated '…Nico's father.' Glancing at Sergio, she explained, 'Miss Morris is the senior play-worker at Little Acorns Nursery.'

'I'm delighted to meet you, Miss Morris,' Sergio murmured in his sexy accent that brought Kristen's skin out in goose-bumps. And clearly she was not the only woman to be bowled over by his mega-watt charm, she thought ruefully as she noticed Lizzie's cheeks turn pink.

'Please call me Lizzie, Mr Castellano,' the play-worker said rather breathlessly. 'May I say it's so nice to finally meet Nico's father. Would you like to come into the office while Kristen makes sure Nico is settled?'

'Thank you—Lizzie. And do please call me Sergio.'

'Oh, yes…certainly.'

Leaving the flustered play-worker with Sergio, Kristen went to find Nico. He was sitting on a bean-bag and looked so disconsolate that her heart ached. 'How about playing with the train set?' she suggested.

He shook his head, and the sight of tears sliding down his cheeks evoked the usual feeling of guilt that she was leaving him. But, remembering Lizzie's advice to keep goodbyes brief, she leaned down and dropped a kiss onto his cheek. 'Have a lovely day and I'll come back very soon.'

His sobs followed her as she hurried out of the playroom and into the corridor. Lizzie emerged from the office, followed by Sergio, who frowned when he heard Nico crying. 'Are you sure he isn't being bullied?' he asked tersely.

Lizzie looked shocked. 'Oh, no! He just gets upset when he's separated from his mother, but his tears don't last for long. It's a fairly common reaction with children of his age,' she explained. 'And Nico is particularly sensitive at the moment. But don't worry. I'll take good care of him.'

It was a pity that Kristen didn't seem to feel the same

concern for her son that the play-worker did, Sergio thought darkly as they left the nursery and walked back to the car. The sound of his son's sobs affected him deeply and brought back memories of how as a little boy he had often wept silently into his pillow at night, afraid that if he made a noise he would anger his mother. He had cried because he missed his father.

'As soon as my lawyers can arrange a custody hearing I intend to claim my legal rights to my son,' he informed Kristen abruptly. 'Nico belongs in Sicily with me.'

Shock caused the colour to drain from Kristen's face. 'Don't be ridiculous. He's just a baby. No court would allow you to take him away from his mother.' She bit her lip. 'We must put Nico's welfare first. I don't want him upset in any way.'

'I saw when you walked away from him while he was crying how concerned you are for his emotional welfare,' Sergio said with icy sarcasm. Hearing Nico crying had aroused his protective instincts and he was tempted to stride back into the nursery and snatch his little son into his arms. It was a father's duty to protect his child—a duty his own father had failed to do. But he would not fail his son, Sergio vowed grimly. Kristen did not seem to care overmuch about Nico and he was sure the boy would be far happier living with him.

In the car Kristen gave directions to the driver on how to reach her work while Sergio called his PR manager.

'Enzo will give a statement to the press and explain that we have no personal involvement,' he told her when he ended the call. 'It's rather ironic, considering that we have a child, but I want to keep Nico out of the media spotlight for as long as possible.'

'I understand if you want a relationship with Nico,'

Kristen said huskily. 'But surely it would be better for him if we come to an amicable arrangement about when you can visit him rather than arguing over who should have custody of him.'

'I don't want to visit him.' Sergio turned his gaze from the rain lashing the car window and looked into Kristen's bright blue eyes. 'I want my son to live with me so that I can be a proper father to him.' There was a curious fervency in his voice as he continued, 'I want to tuck Nico into bed every night and eat breakfast with him every morning. I want to kick a football with him and take him swimming.' He shot her a glance. 'Have you taught him to swim?'

'Not yet,' Kristen admitted. 'There isn't a public pool near to where we live, and weekends go so quickly. He's only three, for goodness' sake,' she said tersely when Sergio frowned.

'My niece is only a year older than Nico, but Rosa has been able to swim virtually since she learned to walk.'

His criticism of her mothering skills rankled. 'If I could afford for Nico to live in a house with its own private pool, I've no doubt he would be able to swim like a fish,' she snapped.

'If I had known I had a son, he would have grown up from birth at my house on the Castallano estate and I would have taught him to swim in my pool.'

Kristen's angry gaze clashed with Sergio's furious glare. 'You keep saying you would have supported him, but I don't understand how you would have done. You were married when Nico was born. How could he have lived with you in Sicily? Why did your marriage end, anyway?' She could not deny her curiosity. 'Did your wife leave you or…'

'She died.'

'I…I'm sorry,' she whispered, shocked as much by the

revelation as by the complete lack of emotion in Sergio's voice. She wanted to ask him: when? How? For the past four years she had been haunted by the photo she had seen in a magazine of the beautiful woman Sergio had married. She had been jealous, Kristen admitted to herself.

'Did you love her?' She could not hold back the question that had burned inside her for four years.

'It's none of your business.'

His reply was polite but dismissive and she flushed, hating herself for her curiosity and him for his arrogance. Determined not to risk another put-down, she stared out of the window and willed the traffic jam to clear before she was any later for work.

'I'm surprised that I have never seen your name mentioned by the media.'

Puzzled by the statement, she glanced at him. 'Why on earth should I be of interest to anyone?'

'Four years ago you were regarded as one of the best gymnasts in the UK and were tipped to win a gold medal at the world championships. But after you left Sicily and returned to England you seemed to disappear from the sport.' Sergio's jaw hardened. 'I realise now that you must have taken a break from training and competitions while you were pregnant. But didn't you return to gymnastics after Nico was born?'

Kristen shook her head. 'I never competed again after I had him. I gave up gymnastics completely. It wasn't possible to combine the hours of training necessary to compete at world-class level with being a mother,' she explained when she saw the surprise in Sergio's eyes.

'But gymnastics meant the world to you.'

'Nico is my world now,' she said simply. 'Being his mother is more important to me than anything.'

She turned her head to the window to watch the traffic crawling along Tottenham Court Road, and missed the sharp look Sergio gave her. 'It will be quicker for me to walk the rest of the way to work. The clinic isn't far from here.'

Sergio asked the driver to pull over, but as Kristen was about to step out of the car he put his hand on her arm. 'Here's my phone number in case you need to get hold of me. I'll meet you at Nico's nursery at five-thirty to drive you both home.'

She took the business card he handed her and shoved it into her pocket. 'There's no need for you to come to the nursery. I usually take Nico to the park on the way home.'

'Then I'll bring a football and we will stop off at the park. I'm looking forward to being able to play with my son.'

'Fine.' She looked away from the challenge in his eyes, determined not to let him see how scared she felt that he might truly try to win custody of Nico. Sergio could easily afford the best lawyers, but heaven knew how she would afford to pay legal costs if there was a lengthy court case. The possibility that she could be forced to give up her son filled Kristen with dread.

CHAPTER FIVE

THE DAY HAD begun badly and grew steadily worse. Arriving late for work meant that Kristen missed her first appointment and spent all day playing catch-up and trying to rearrange physiotherapy sessions.

After work she hurried to the station and squashed herself into a packed carriage. But a few minutes into the journey the Tube train ground to a halt in the tunnel and the lights flickered off, plunging the carriages into darkness. Breakdowns on the underground system happened rarely and when the train did not move after five minutes a few passengers started to become agitated. Kristen checked her phone, knowing it was unlikely she would pick up a network connection deep underground. There was nothing anyone could do except wait in the darkness but, as the minutes stretched to ten, fifteen, twenty, her tension grew as it became clear that she would be late to pick Nico up from nursery.

At five twenty-five that afternoon, Sergio parked outside Little Acorns Nursery and studied the group of parents already gathered outside the door of the building. Kristen had not arrived yet, but he was early. Five minutes later when the nursery door opened and the parents filed in she still had not shown up. Knowing that Nico was waiting, Sergio walked inside and was greeted by Lizzie Morris.

'Hi! Kristen isn't here yet, but she comes straight from work and sometimes she is a few minutes late.' Lizzie smiled. 'You can wait with Nico if you want. I'm sure he'll be pleased to see you.'

Nico was sitting in the book corner, his eyes focused intently on the door. A flash of instant recognition crossed his face when he saw Sergio and he gave a tentative smile that tugged on Sergio's heart.

'Mummy's not here.' The smile faded and Nico's bottom lip trembled.

'She will be here soon,' Sergio reassured him gently. 'While we wait for her shall I read you a story?'

He was rewarded with another smile that stole his breath. *Dio*, his son was beautiful. He couldn't take his eyes from the little boy's face. Nico's features were like his own in miniature, although he had his mother's nose, Sergio noted. He opened the book that Nico had handed him and began to read in a voice that wasn't quite steady.

Trapped on the Tube train, Kristen's tension escalated with every passing minute. The staff would look after Nico until she arrived, she reassured herself. Lizzie would realise there must be a good reason why she was unable to phone and explain why she was delayed. But imagining Nico's disappointed face when she didn't walk through the door with the other parents brought tears to her eyes and she felt sick with worry.

Eventually the fault on the underground line was repaired, but by the time she raced out of the station and was able to phone the nursery she was forty-five minutes late and frantic.

'Is Nico okay? Tell him I'll be there in a couple of minutes,' she said to Lizzie, panting as she ran along the street.

'Kristen, calm down. Nico's fine. His father took him.'

'W…what?' By now Kristen had arrived at the nursery but, on hearing Lizzie's shocking news, she slowed her pace and walked into the building, feeling as though her heart was about to explode out of her chest. 'What do you mean his father took him?'

'Sergio arrived just before five-thirty and he waited around for a while, but we both realised that you must have got held up at work. I explained that it had happened on a couple of previous occasions,' Lizzie said guilelessly. 'Luckily he said he would take Nico with him.' Lizzie seemed unaware of Kristen's tension and smiled cheerfully. 'Sergio filled out a parent/guardian form when he came in with you this morning. If he hadn't, of course, I wouldn't have been able to allow him to take Nico. But he was fine about it, and Nico was really excited to go in Sergio's car. Mind you, I'd be pretty excited about travelling in a Jaguar XJ. It's a gorgeous car.'

Lizzie stopped short of saying that Sergio was equally gorgeous, but Kristen guessed from the nursery assistant's pink cheeks that she had been bowled over by a surfeit of Sicilian charm. Hurrying out of the nursery, she pulled Sergio's business card from her jacket pocket and entered his number into her phone with shaking fingers. *Pick up, pick up…* Her imagination went into overdrive and she felt sick with terror that Sergio might have taken Nico out of the country on his private plane. She had read about so-called tug-of-love cases where children had been taken abroad by one parent without the other parent's consent. *What if Sergio disappeared with Nico and she never saw her little boy again?*

'Castellano.' Sergio finally answered the call and at

the sound of his deep voice Kristen's knees almost gave way with relief.

'What have you done with Nico? Where is he…?'

Sergio's reply was terse. 'I haven't *done* anything with him. I simply collected him from nursery when you failed to show up and brought him back to my hotel. He's perfectly okay, although he was upset that you weren't there to pick him up,' he told her coldly. 'I understand from Lizzie Morris that today is not the first time you have been late.'

'There have only been two other occasions,' Kristen defended herself. 'And, like today, they were not my fault. The train broke down in the tunnel and I couldn't phone…'

'I really think you should have tried harder to get to Nico on time,' Sergio interrupted her. 'Have you any idea what it's like to be the only child left waiting to be collected? The fear he must have felt that you weren't coming for him?'

His words scraped Kristen's already raw feeling of guilt. She had a strange sense that Sergio was speaking from personal experience—as if knew what it felt like to be a scared little boy waiting for his mother to show up. But she told herself she must be imagining things. The Castellano family was hugely wealthy and he must have enjoyed a privileged childhood. He certainly didn't know what it was like to be a single working mother with all the responsibility that entailed, she thought grimly. His complete lack of understanding of her situation made her want to scream.

'You're a bloody expert in child psychology, I suppose,' she said grittily. 'Of course I feel terrible that I let Nico down.' Tears suddenly filled her eyes and her throat closed up. 'Thank you for being there for him,' she choked. 'I'll come to the Hotel Royale to collect him, but it might take me a while because the trains are busy during the rush-hour.'

'Stay where you are and I'll send the car for you.'

Sergio cut the call before Kristen could argue. He always had to be in control of every situation, she thought grimly. His wealth gave him power, but it was more than money; his supreme confidence and arrogant self-assurance made him a commanding and authoritative figure—and his steely control over his emotions would make him a dangerous enemy.

The penthouse suite of the Hotel Royale looked very different from the last time Kristen had visited. On Friday evening the elegant sitting room had been immaculately tidy, but now it resembled a toy shop. Numerous boxes and torn wrapping paper littered the carpet; there was a train track complete with model trains in one corner, an enormous tractor, a robot figure and a model garage filled with toy cars.

Nico was sitting on the floor, pushing cars along a plastic roadway and making an engine sound. He barely looked up when Kristen walked in, before he returned to his game sending cars along the track to Sergio, who was pushing them back to him.

The biggest surprise for Kristen was to see Sergio stretched out on the floor, apparently absorbed in playing with the little boy. His tie was draped over the arm of a chair and his shirtsleeves were rolled up, revealing his tanned forearms covered with a mass of dark hairs. He looked so big next to Nico, yet Kristen noted with a pang the close physical resemblance between the man and the child.

She paused in the doorway, feeling strangely awkward and excluded. Usually when she met Nico at nursery he would hurtle into her arms and she would cuddle him. But, although he glanced at her again, he remained on the floor with Sergio.

'Mummy, I've got lots of cars.'

'So I see.' Telling herself to stop being so stupid, she smiled and walked over to kneel down next to him. Immediately she was conscious of Sergio's cool scrutiny. 'Anyone would think it's Christmas,' she murmured drily. 'You must have bought an entire toy shop.'

'I have three Christmases to make up for.' He didn't try to hide the bitterness in his voice. Kristen flushed and quickly focused her attention on Nico.

'It looks like you're having fun.'

'You didn't come.' Nico lifted his chocolate button eyes to her. 'I looked and looked for you, Mummy.'

Kristen swallowed. 'I'm sorry, sweetheart. The train broke down and got stuck in a tunnel. It wasn't very nice.' Her voice shook. She felt claustrophobic on the Tube at the best of times, and she had felt panicky and terrified while she had been trapped underground.

'My daddy came.'

Sweet heaven! She shot Sergio a startled look and met his bland gaze. Forcing a smile for Nico, she said lightly, 'Yes, it was very kind of him to collect you from nursery, wasn't it?'

Nico nodded. 'I went in my daddy's big car.'

Kristen knew she shouldn't be surprised by Nico's uncomplicated acceptance of the situation. He was aware that his friends at nursery had daddies and he was bound to be fascinated by Sergio. But she was angry that Sergio had revealed his identity without checking with her first.

Leaving Nico to his game, she walked across the room and sank down on the sofa before her legs gave way. Today had been one unpleasant shock after another.

Sergio followed her and gave an impatient frown as he correctly read her mind. 'What did you expect me to do?

Surely it's better for him to know that I'm his father rather than a stranger?'

She bit her lip. 'I guess so.'

'*Santa Madre!* It would be nice if you could help to make this easier for his sake.'

Sergio's jaw clenched as he sought to control his temper. He had been furious when Kristen had failed to show up to collect Nico, and also disappointed. She had sounded so genuine when she had told him that Nico meant the world to her. He had almost been taken in by her and believed that she was more caring than his own mother had been.

At the nursery he had watched Nico become increasingly upset as he had waited for Kristen, and Sergio's heart had ached for the little boy. It had brought back memories of how his mother had regularly been late to pick him up from the after-school club she had sent him to every day. On several occasions she had forgotten him completely, until one of the staff had phoned her to remind her about her son. Sergio remembered the cramping fear in his gut that one day his mother simply would not show up. What would happen to him then? he had wondered. Who would take care of him? He had given up hoping that his father would come and take him back to Sicily.

He had brought Nico back to the hotel, convinced that Kristen was irresponsible and did not deserve to have custody of their son. But, glancing at her pale face, he recalled how her voice had trembled when she had explained how she had been trapped on a Tube train, and his anger lessened. Her physiotherapist's uniform of navy trousers and white jacket gave her a professional air but she still looked heartbreakingly young with her long golden hair falling around her shoulders. The purple smudges beneath her eyes indicated that she had slept as badly as he had for the past three nights.

Had memories of making love with him kept her awake until the early hours? Perhaps, like him, she could not forget the intense passion that had blazed between them three nights ago. He had never wanted any woman as badly as he had wanted Kristen. And he still desired her, Sergio acknowledged grimly. Much as he might resent the fact, he could not deny the truth.

When she moved her head her hair shimmered like a silk curtain and he could smell the lemony scent of shampoo. A button on her uniform had popped open so that he could glimpse the curve of her breasts beneath her semi-transparent bra. Heat flared in his groin and he shifted his position to try and ease the throb of his arousal.

Just then she glanced at him from beneath her long lashes and as their eyes met and held, something unspoken passed between them. If they had been alone he would have carried her into the bedroom—and she would have let him. It was the one thing he was certain of.

But they were not alone. He jerked his gaze from her and focused on his son—the child she had kept secret from him. Nico was still playing with the toy cars, his expression utterly absorbed as he chatted to himself in his sweet childish voice. A shaft of golden evening sunshine slanted through the window and fingered the little boy's dark curls.

'Dio!' Sergio exhaled raggedly as he felt an arrow pierce his heart. 'How could you have hidden him from me?' he asked Kristen in a tortured voice. 'He is my child. My blood runs through his veins. You must have known I would want to be part of his life.'

She shook her head, genuinely shocked by the raw emotion in his voice.

'You didn't give me that impression in the hospital. After I'd had the miscarriage, you said it was for the best that I had lost the baby…and I took that to mean you didn't want a child.' Her voice shook. 'I thought you were relieved that I was no longer pregnant. And so when I discovered weeks later that I was still carrying your child, I assumed that you wouldn't welcome the news.'

Sergio had stiffened and he looked almost grey beneath his tan. 'I certainly did not feel relieved that you had lost our child. That day at the hospital…' He swallowed convulsively. 'You misunderstood me. One of the nurses had told me that miscarriages often occurred if the baby was not developing properly. She also said that women sometimes blamed themselves when they lost a child, and it was important I should reassure you that you could not have prevented what had happened.

'That was why I said that perhaps it had been for the best. You were so upset, and I didn't know how else to try and comfort you. You were crying and you needed me to be strong…not to cry too,' he said raggedly.

'I was so shocked when the doctor told me I was pregnant, and then in the same sentence that I had miscarried the baby,' Kristen whispered. She stared at Sergio. 'I had no idea that you were sad about it. Did you really feel like crying?' It was hard to believe that he could have been as deeply affected by the loss of their baby as she had.

'The knowledge that we had lost something so precious and irreplaceable felt like a body blow. At first I couldn't take it in. We had created a new life, but tragically our child was not destined to live.'

Sergio watched Nico playing. 'But we did create a new life after all,' he said so softly that Kristen only just caught his words. 'I still can't quite believe that this beautiful little boy is my son.'

She bit her lip. 'I often think about the other baby, and I wonder what Nico's brother or sister would have been like. I feel so lucky to have him, but I mourn for his twin and, although it's selfish, I wish I could have had them both.' She glanced at Sergio. 'I've heard that the bond between twins is unique. Do you feel especially close to your twin brother?'

He shrugged. 'I did not grow up with Salvatore, and when we met again after being separated for many years we did not have a close relationship.'

She gave him a startled look. 'Why didn't you grow up together?'

'My parents split up when Salvatore and I were five years old. My mother returned to her native New York and she took me with her.'

Kristen frowned. 'It seems a strange decision to have separated you from your brother. You told me that your parents had divorced when you were young, but I assumed that you and Salvatore grew up in Sicily with your father.'

'I did not discover until I was much older that my father had been awarded custody of both of us,' he told her emotionlessly. 'My mother snatched me and took me to America. My father tried to get me back but...' He broke off and shrugged.

How hard had Tito really fought for his return? Sergio brooded. Surely in the ten years that he had lived in the US his father could have done more to force his mother to allow him to return to Sicily? The thought was a poison that continually festered in his mind. The only answer as far as he could see was that Tito had not loved him as much as he had loved Salvatore.

'I suppose she couldn't bear to lose both of her children.' Privately, Kristen wondered how Sergio's mother could have taken him away from his brother and broken the special bond between the twin boys.

Sergio's expression became sardonic. 'The only reason she took me was to get at my father. Their relationship was a constant power struggle both before and after they divorced. Patti didn't actually want me. She was busy pursuing an acting career and having a child around was hugely inconvenient.'

Kristen was startled by the bitterness in his voice. 'I'm sure she didn't think that,' she murmured, not knowing what else to say. The coldness in his eyes sent a shiver through her. Four years ago she had thought she had known him, but clearly there were secrets in his past that might explain why he kept such a tight rein on his emotions.

She glanced at her watch and jumped to her feet. 'I must take Nico home. He needs his dinner and a bath before bed.'

'He's already eaten. I asked the chef to prepare him grilled chicken and vegetables and he ate most of his dinner.' Sergio gave her a piercing glance. 'He looks too thin and I am concerned that he is underweight. I think he should be checked over by a doctor.'

'He has been off his food recently,' Kristen admitted, 'but he's perfectly healthy.'

'Nevertheless, I have made an appointment for him to see a top paediatrician in Harley Street tomorrow morning.'

'There's no need.' Her temper simmered at his implication that she didn't take enough care of her son but, faced with Sergio's implacable expression, Kristen swallowed her irritation. It was pointless to argue over a minor issue when the vital question of who would have custody of Nico was yet to be resolved.

'As for tonight,' Sergio continued, 'he can stay here at the hotel. I have already had the second bedroom in my suite prepared for him.'

A tight knot of tension formed in Kristen's stomach

when she realised that she was not included in the invitation. 'I'm not going to leave Nico with you.'

'Why not? I am his father.' His eyes glittered. '*Dio*, is one night, when you have had him to yourself for the past three years, too much to ask for?'

'Mummy, where's Hippo?'

Nico's voice cut through the simmering atmosphere and Kristen tore her eyes from Sergio's angry face and focused on her son.

'He's at home, sweetheart. Would you like to go and find him?'

Relief washed over her when Nico nodded. She could tell that he was tired, and when he climbed onto her lap and put his head on her shoulder she cuddled him. He was her baby and she would fight to the death for him. She glanced at Sergio and flushed at the sardonic expression in his eyes.

'Hippo is his favourite toy,' she explained. 'He takes it to bed with him every night.'

'In that case I'd better drive you both home,' he said coolly. 'I don't want to upset Nico. But I warn you, *cara*,' he added in a dangerously soft voice, 'don't try to play games with me.'

When Sergio parked outside Kristen's small terraced house she noticed, as he no doubt did, that the front door badly needed a coat of paint. It was one of many jobs that she never had time to do, she thought with a sigh. Walking into the house, she was horribly conscious that the wallpaper in the hallway was peeling. Decorating was another job on the to-do list that lack of time and her tight budget did not stretch to. Since her mum had died she had been getting by, surviving, but not really living, she acknowledged. Grief had sapped her energy and dulled her spirit and it was a bitter irony that seeing Sergio again had made her feel more alive than she had done in months.

Sergio followed her into the kitchen and she saw him frown at the sight of the empty wine bottles on the table. The clothes rack was draped with her underwear and the sink was full of dirty dishes that she hadn't had time to wash up in the rush to get out that morning. Fortunately the living room was reasonably tidy, although shabby, Kristen acknowledged. It was funny how she had never noticed how worn the carpet was until now, and the red wine stain—courtesy of Steph spilling her drink the previous evening—added to the room's neglected air.

Sergio had carried Nico in from the car, and Kristen felt a tug of possessiveness at the sight of the little boy resting his dark curls on his father's shoulder. He was *her* baby.

'I'll take him straight up for his bath. I expect you want to get back to the hotel.'

'I'm not in any rush.' Sergio's jaw tightened at her unsubtle attempt to dismiss him. 'We need to talk.'

Had four words ever sounded so ominous? Kristen watched Sergio glance disparagingly around the room. It was on the tip of her tongue to point out that, unlike him, she could not afford to buy a luxury mansion in Mayfair, which the newspaper had reported he was currently purchasing, but she thought better of it and led Nico up the stairs.

Left alone in the dismal sitting room, Sergio recalled the empty wine bottles in the kitchen and almost gave in to the urge to chase after his son, snatch him into his arms and take him to Sicily immediately. The house was in dire need of renovation, and it was apparent that Kristen had had a party recently—unless she had drunk several bottles of wine herself.

He grimaced. His mother had preferred gin and, even

though it was years since his childhood, he couldn't bear the smell of it. Patti's temperament had been unpredictable at the best of times and alcohol had made her either maudlin or cruel. Unfortunately there had been no way of telling what mood she would be in and, as a small boy not much older than Nico, Sergio had felt constantly on edge, fearful of angering his mother and provoking her violent temper.

A loud scream dragged him from his thoughts. The sound of a child's hysterical sobs chilled Sergio's blood and he took the stairs two at a time and burst into the bathroom to find Nico—not being beaten, as he had wildly imagined—but in the throes of a full-blown tantrum while Kristen endeavoured to wash his hair.

She was drenched, and one part of Sergio's mind registered that her white tunic top was virtually see-through and he could clearly make out the firm swell of her breasts beneath her uniform.

'He hates having his hair washed,' she explained somewhat unnecessarily as Nico wriggled out of her grasp and covered his head with his hands.

'*No,* Mummy,' the little boy yelled furiously.

Sergio struggled to prevent his lips from twitching when he recognised that his son had inherited his hot temper. 'Does he always react like this?' he murmured.

'Every bath-time,' Kristen told him wearily. She was unaware that Sergio had frowned because he had glimpsed the shimmer of tears in her eyes. Her shoulders slumped as she waited for him to criticize her once again. He clearly thought she was a useless mother, and maybe he was right, she thought miserably. Nico was adorable, but he was also a strong-willed little boy and she was worried that if she didn't learn how to deal with his tantrums he would become wilful. If only her mum was still here, she thought, swallowing the lump in her throat. Kathleen had been brilliant with Nico and Kristen missed her advice and guidance.

She stiffened when Sergio knelt down beside her in front of the bath. He seemed unconcerned that the floor was wet and, to her surprise, he rolled up his shirtsleeves. But his next comment surprised her even more.

'It must be tough working full-time as well as bringing up Nico on your own without any help,' he said quietly.

Kristen almost believed that he understood how tired and overwhelmed she felt sometimes, but then she remembered his threat to seek custody of Nico. No doubt he would seize on an admission that she found being a single mother challenging.

'I manage okay,' she told him shortly. 'I don't need anyone's help.'

Studying Nico's mutinous expression, Sergio was inclined to disagree with her, but he sensed she was on edge and refrained from pointing out that once he had gained custody of his son she would be free to concentrate on her career.

He smiled at Nico. 'I'll make a deal with you. If I let you wash my hair, will you let me wash yours?'

Intrigued, the little boy nodded. Sergio bent his head over the bath and, with a squeal of laughter, Nico filled a plastic jug with water and tipped it over his father's hair. Within seconds Sergio's shirt was soaked through, but Kristen could not help but be impressed with his patience with Nico and, to her astonishment, the little boy didn't make a fuss when it was his turn to have his hair washed.

'He's really taken to you,' she said gruffly as she lifted Nico out of the bath and wrapped a towel around him.

'Why are you surprised? He is my son and as much a part of me as he is of you.' Sergio watched Nico scamper along the hallway to his bedroom and felt an almost painful surge of love for his child. He had missed so much. The precious first days, weeks and months of his son's life were gone for ever and he wanted to weep for what he had lost. But there was no point in looking backwards. The future was what mattered, and he was determined that he would not be denied another day of Nico's life.

To Kristen's consternation, Sergio unbuttoned his wet shirt and slipped it off, revealing his tanned torso and the hard ridges of his abdominal muscles.

'I'm afraid I don't have a tumble dryer,' she mumbled, knowing she should look away, but her eyes were locked on the mouth-watering view of his gorgeous half-naked body.

'No matter, I always keep spare clothes in the car.' He picked up a towel and blotted the moisture from the whorls of dark hairs covering his chest. Kristen drew a sharp breath when she saw several red scratch marks on his shoulders.

Following her gaze, Sergio's mouth curved into an amused smile. 'You were a wild-cat the other night, *cara*.'

'That wasn't me…' She came to an abrupt halt, colour scalding her cheeks as a memory of clinging to his sweat-slicked shoulders and raking her nails over his skin when he had brought her to a mind-blowing orgasm flooded her mind. Dear heaven, she had behaved like a wanton creature in his arms.

The sultry gleam in his eyes warned her that he had a total recall of making love to her three nights ago. Her pulse leapt and involuntarily she swayed towards him. Her senses were swamped by his maleness—a mixture of aftershave and the indefinable scent of pheromones. Sexual awareness crackled in the tiny bathroom. She watched his eyes darken and held her breath as he dipped his head towards her.

'*Mummy...*'

Kristen assured herself that she was relieved by Nico's timely interruption. 'I'd better go and see to him,' she said jerkily and shot out of the bathroom, followed by Sergio's mocking laughter.

CHAPTER SIX

WHEN KRISTEN WENT downstairs after she had tucked Nico into bed there was no sign of Sergio and she assumed he had gone back to his hotel. She couldn't understand why she felt deflated. A reprieve from his threatened talk could only be a good thing. But as she filled the sink with water to begin the washing-up he strolled into the kitchen, still bare-chested, and carrying a holdall that she guessed he had collected from his car. Heaven knew what her neighbours must think! She tried to ignore the urgent thud of her heart as he opened the bag and took out a T-shirt, which he pulled over his head.

Unfortunately he looked no less sexy in the tight-fitting black shirt that emphasised his muscular physique. He would look good wearing a bin bag, Kristen thought ruefully. He unsettled her and she wished he would go away and give her some space.

'I realise we have things to discuss, but I'm tired tonight. It's been a difficult day,' she muttered, not sure whether to laugh or cry at the understatement. 'Do you want to come over tomorrow evening instead?'

Sergio gave her a piercing glance and noted that the shadows beneath her eyes had darkened to purple bruises. Her delicate features were drawn and she looked fragile and barely any older than she had done four years ago. The first time he had seen her, she had been dancing on the beach, he remembered. Actually, she had been practising her gymnastics floor routine, she had explained, blushing with embarrassment when she had realised she'd had an audience. Sergio had been entranced by her slender, graceful body and her fey beauty. She had touched his soul in a way no other woman had ever done. But he had no intention of succumbing to her magic again, certainly not now he had discovered that she had kept his son from him.

'You seem to be under the misapprehension that I am going somewhere, but I'm not leaving,' he said curtly. 'I want to see my son first thing in the morning.' Sensing that she was about to argue, his expression hardened. 'The other reason I'm going to spend the night here is to make sure you don't disappear with Nico.'

'I wouldn't do that,' Kristen said sharply, stung by his scathing tone.

'You hid him from me for three years,' he reminded her coldly.

She shook her head, despairing that she would ever make him understand why she had acted as she had. 'I truly believed you would not want him. When we were together you constantly told me you didn't want a committed relationship, and having a child is a massive commitment.' Faced with his implacable expression, she sighed and gave up. 'Anyway, there's nowhere for you to sleep. The house only has two bedrooms, and Nico's room is too small for you to share with him.'

'Then I guess I'll have to share with you.'

Unexpectedly, Sergio smiled, revealing his gleaming white teeth. Kristen caught her breath as she was instantly transported back to the first time she had met him on the beach in Sicily. He had been wearing running shorts and a vest top that had shown off his tanned, athletic body.

With his dark hair falling into his chocolate-brown eyes, he had been the sexiest man she had ever laid eyes on, and when he had smiled she had been utterly blown away by him. They had become lovers within days of that first encounter, she remembered. Four years on, the attraction between them was still potent and three nights ago it had blazed into an inferno. But Kristen knew she couldn't risk her emotional security by sleeping with him again.

'I'd rather share my bed with the devil,' she said tartly, desperate to disguise the ache of tears in her voice as she was overwhelmed by memories of the past.

His brows rose. 'I didn't get that impression on Friday night.'

She flushed. 'That was a mistake. The champagne went to my head.'

'You only had one glass.' He gave her a speculative look. 'I take it you haven't been drinking champagne today?'

'Of course not. I was at work, and then trapped on a Tube train for nearly an hour,' she reminded him drily.

'In that case, my experiment should reveal the truth.'

Kristen had not been aware of Sergio moving, but suddenly he was far too close for comfort and, as he reached behind her and cupped her nape, she realised too late that she had walked into a trap.

'Don't...' Her voice faltered as his head swooped and his warm breath feathered her lips.

'I am about to prove that you are a little liar, *cara*,' he threatened softly, before he stifled her protest by slanting his mouth over hers.

It was no gentle seduction. His lips were firm and demanding, taking without mercy as he twined his fingers in her hair and hauled her against him, trapping her with his arms, which felt like bands of steel while he ravished her tender mouth.

Kristen's determination to resist him was dissolving in the honeyed sweetness of his kiss. It felt so good when she had been starved of him for so long. It would be so easy to sink into him and give in to his sensual mastery. Summoning her willpower, she attempted to push against his rock-hard chest, but it was futile. She couldn't escape him, nor could she deny the hot tide of desire that poured through her veins and pooled between her thighs.

With a soft moan, she opened her mouth for him and trembled when he slid his tongue between her lips. Reality faded, just as it had done three nights ago at the hotel. But suddenly, shockingly, he lifted his head and stared down at her, and the triumphant gleam in his eyes acted like an ice-cold shower on her heated flesh.

'Don't ever lie to me again, Kristen. Next time I won't stop at kissing you,' he warned. His mouth curled in self-disgust as he stepped away from her and raked a hand through his hair. 'Believe me, I resent the wildfire attraction between us as much as you do, but it's there and we will have to deal with it because I'm not going to go away. Nico is a part of both of us and we will be forever linked by him.'

His emotive words shook Kristen and tears filled her eyes. Sergio gave her a piercing look but, when she made no response, he said, 'I'll sleep on the sofa tonight, and tomorrow we'll discuss the best way we can bring up our son.' He glanced around the untidy kitchen and his jaw hardened. 'This place is far from ideal,' he said disparagingly.

Kristen felt a stab of fear. Surely he wouldn't be able to state that she was an unfit mother just because she hadn't had time to do the washing-up?

'I'll go and find some bedding,' she mumbled, seizing the excuse to get away from him while thoughts whirled around her head. She ran upstairs and paused on the landing to peep into Nico's room. He had flung back the covers as he usually did and was cuddling Hippo. He looked utterly adorable with his halo of dark curls framing his face and his long eyelashes fanned out on his cheeks. Intense love surged up inside her. She would never give her little boy up, she vowed fiercely. She was deeply suspicious of Sergio's insistence that he wanted to be involved with his son. The man she had known four years ago had been the ultimate commitment-phobe and it would take a lot to convince her that he had changed. Her biggest fear was that he would form a bond with Nico and then walk away when the novelty of fatherhood had faded.

She took a blanket and spare pillow from the hall cupboard, and then went into her bedroom to change out of her uniform, which felt uncomfortably damp after her attempts to wash Nico's hair. Furious with herself for being tempted to wear her new lilac silky top that clung in all the right places, she pulled on jeans and an old T-shirt and quickly brushed her hair, but resisted the urge to put on a bit of make-up. It wasn't as if she wanted to make herself look attractive for Sergio, she reminded herself firmly.

A tantalising aroma of spicy food met her as she walked into the kitchen, reminding her that she had been too busy to eat lunch. Sergio was opening cartons of take-away food. He had found plates and cutlery, and she saw that he had washed up the breakfast bowls.

'I ordered Thai,' he said, glancing at her. 'I remembered you like it and I'm guessing you haven't eaten tonight. There's nothing in the fridge except for a couple of out-of-date yoghurts. What had you planned to give Nico for dinner?'

She prickled at the implied criticism in his voice. 'I was going to call in at the supermarket on the way home from nursery. Here's your bedding,' she murmured, handing him the pillow and blanket.

He gave her a sardonic look when he felt the coarse woollen blanket. 'I've heard of monks wearing hair shirts. Have you decided that I should serve some sort of penance?' he queried drily.

She flushed. 'You could always go back to your hotel.'

'And give you an opportunity to steal Nico away?' He gave a bitter laugh. 'Not a chance, Krissie.'

His use of the nickname that only he had ever called her by twisted a knife in Kristen's heart, but somehow she managed to give a shrug as she sat down and began to help herself to food. Sergio opened a bottle of red wine that she assumed had been delivered with the meal, but when he went to fill her glass she shook her head.

'Not for me, thanks. I rarely drink wine.'

His brows rose. 'Then how do you explain the half a dozen empty bottles that I put in the recycling bin?'

'A few of my girlfriends came over last night. One of them has just gone through an acrimonious divorce and she wanted to celebrate being free and single again.'

'And where was Nico while this drunken party was going on?'

'*It wasn't a drunken party!*' She glared at him. 'The girls just had a few drinks. Nico was tucked up safely in bed, and I didn't touch any alcohol. I am a responsible parent.'

'What about on Friday evening?' Sergio pressed. 'Where was Nico while you were in my bed?'

Kristen choked on a prawn ball. 'I certainly didn't leave him on his own, if that's what you're implying. My neighbour babysat. Nico was in bed asleep before I left, but he knows Sally very well, and she adores him.'

'You still haven't explained why you were pretending to be a waitress at the party.'

'The waitress bit was a misunderstanding.' Kristen's appetite suddenly disappeared. Sergio had finished his meal and she collected up the plates and carried them over to the sink. 'Do you want to go into the sitting room while I make some coffee? There are a few photo albums with pictures of Nico in the bureau. Feel free to take a look at them.'

She could tell he was curious to know why she was determined to change the subject of her visit to the Hotel Royale, but to her relief he made no comment as he strolled out of the kitchen.

Five minutes later, when Kristen carried a tray into the sitting room, she found Sergio inspecting her huge array of gymnastics medals and trophies that she kept in a glass cabinet.

He turned to her and took the cup of coffee she handed him. 'Do you ever resent that you gave up your sport for Nico?'

'Not at all, although I can't deny that I sometimes wonder whether I would have been good enough to win a world championship title,' Kristen replied honestly.

'So when you returned to England and discovered you were still expecting, it didn't cross your mind to end the pregnancy?'

She drew a sharp breath, 'Of course not. I was devastated when I had a miscarriage, and to be told that I was going to have a baby after all was wonderful—it felt like a miracle. How could you think I might not have wanted our child?' She couldn't disguise the tremor of hurt in her voice.

It probably had something to do with the fact that when

he had been a child his mother had frequently told him she had not planned to fall pregnant with him and his twin brother and wished she'd had a termination, Sergio thought to himself. He shrugged. 'When we met, your pursuit of a gymnastics career bordered on obsessive. You might have considered sacrificing an unplanned pregnancy. After all, you put gymnastics before our relationship.'

'That's not true!' Kristen was stung by the unfairness of his accusation.

'You left me to devote yourself to achieving your dream of sporting glory.'

'I left because you wanted our relationship, such as it was, to be solely on your terms. You demanded that I should give up my life—my gymnastics training, my university studies—to be your mistress, but you refused to make any compromises,' Kristen said hotly. 'The only thing that was important to you was your career. You travelled the world in pursuit of the next deal, the next million pounds to add to your fortune, but you refused to acknowledge that my dreams were important to me.'

She bit her lip. 'Our *relationship* was just about sex as far as you were concerned, wasn't it, Sergio?' Her anger faded as quickly as it had flared and left her with a dull ache in her chest. There was no point in opening up old wounds. 'You asked me to be your mistress, but in the same breath you told me that you were not interested in commitment. What did you expect me to do,' she asked bitterly, 'give up everything I'd worked so hard for, for an affair that might last a few months at most?'

'I couldn't give you what you wanted.' Sergio's voice was emotionless, but Kristen was shocked to see a pained, almost tortured look in his eyes before he brought himself under control and his face became its usual expressionless mask. 'I knew you hoped for more from me—women invariably do,' he said sardonically. 'When you returned to England I realised it was for the best.'

'And so you married someone else.' Kristen felt hurt that he had lumped her with his countless other mistresses and had regarded her as needy just because she had hoped for a more meaningful relationship with him than simply sharing his bed. 'Your Sicilian woman must have been very special for you to have overcome your objection to commitment.'

For a fleeting moment she sensed that he was tempted to talk about his first marriage, but he gave a non-committal shrug.

'Yes, she was.'

He picked up the photo album that he had been looking at earlier and stared at a picture of Nico as a newborn baby. 'He looked so tiny when he was born. What did he weigh?'

'He was a few weeks early and he was just over two kilograms, but I fed him myself and he quickly gained weight.'

Sergio studied the photo, which had clearly been taken in the hospital soon after Kristen had given birth to Nico. She looked very young and scared as she clutched the tiny baby in her arms. Anger burned inside him—anger at her for robbing him of the first years of his son's life, but a greater anger with himself because he had not followed his instincts four years ago and gone after her. She had dented his pride when she had refused to be his mistress, he acknowledged. If he was honest, her rejection had hurt him and it had been the realisation that she made him feel vulnerable that had stopped him from following her to England.

'How did you manage?' he asked harshly. 'Did you have to leave university when you realised you were pregnant?'

'No, I was able to finish my degree before Nico was

born, and afterwards I was lucky to get my current job at the sports injury clinic.'

'It must have been a struggle, though.'

'It hasn't been easy…especially financially,' Kristen admitted.

Sergio wondered why she suddenly seemed nervous. His eyes narrowed on her tense face. 'Why did you come to the Hotel Royale on Friday night?'

Her tongue darted out to lick her dry lips. 'I…came to tell you about Nico.'

'Why now, when you had hidden him from me all this time?'

'I was going to…to ask you for help…a financial contribution for him. You have no idea how expensive bringing up a child is.' Kristen faltered when Sergio's eyes darkened with anger. But when he spoke his voice was tightly controlled.

'You're right. I don't know what it's like to bring up a child, but I wish more than anything that I could have shared the experience of caring for our son from the moment he was born. As it is, I would not have discovered his existence if you had not decided to cash in your most valuable asset. Nico,' he explained when she looked puzzled. 'The knowledge that your child's father is a billionaire must have been too tempting to ignore.' His lip curled. 'How much money did you hope to get from me? Did you plan to demand cash in exchange for allowing me to see my son?'

'*No!*' Kristen was appalled by Sergio's accusation. 'All this time I believed you had a wife in Sicily. But then I saw your picture in a newspaper and read that you were going to marry an Earl's daughter, and I decided to ask you for a small contribution towards Nico's upbringing.'

'So your decision had nothing to do with the fact that you have debts amounting to several thousand pounds, mainly in the form of store credit cards?' Sergio said coldly. 'I saw the pile of letters and final demands for payment from debt-collecting agencies.'

Kristen swallowed. She had forgotten that the folder containing dozens of letters from creditors was in the bureau where she kept the photo albums. 'You had no right to look at my private mail.'

He ignored her and said savagely, 'Suddenly it all makes an obscene kind of sense. You've maxed out on your credit cards buying designer clothes and handbags, and so you've decided to use me as a cash cow to bail you out and assumed you could use Nico as leverage.'

'The situation is not what it seems,' Kristen said huskily.

'Then what is it?'

'It's complicated.'

'No, it's very simple,' Sergio said grimly. 'You want money and I want my son. Name your price and the amount will be transferred into your account within twenty-four hours—with the proviso that you allow me to take Nico to Sicily.'

'Don't be ridiculous…' Kristen broke off when she realised he was deadly serious. 'I'm not going to *sell* him to you. The suggestion is disgusting. The only reason I was going to ask you for money was to spend on him, not for anything else. But I've managed on my own for three years and I'll carry on managing.'

'You call this managing?' Sergio's expression was arrogantly derisive as he glanced around the shabby sitting room. 'I can provide my son with a far better lifestyle than he currently has with you. My lawyer has already started the legal process for me to file for custody of Nico, but it would be better for his sake if we settled out of court and, to that end, I am prepared to make you a generous financial offer.'

'You know what you can do with your offer!' Kristen snapped. Inside, she was shaking, but she refused to let Sergio see how scared she felt. He was not a man to make vain threats and she did not doubt that he had already begun his legal claim for Nico. 'You think you can buy anything you want,' she said bitterly. 'But nothing would persuade me to give Nico up.'

'Everything has a price, *cara*.' Sergio sounded strangely weary. He gave a harsh laugh. 'Was that what Friday night was about? Did you use your delectable body as a sweetener, and once I had succumbed to your magic you intended to offer my son to me in return for hard cash?'

Incensed by his taunt, Kristen reacted instinctively and raised her hand but, before she could make contact with his cheek, he captured her wrist in a vice-like grip.

'I wouldn't,' Sergio advised in a dangerously soft voice. He flung her arm from him and raked his fingers through his hair, feeling disgusted with himself when he saw her white face. He had not intended to frighten her, but for a few seconds blind rage had swept through him. 'We both need to cool down,' he muttered. 'Why don't you go to bed and get some sleep. You look all in. We'll talk again in the morning.'

Not trusting herself to remain in the same room as Sergio when she was tempted to murder him, Kristen swung round and walked out of the room. Sleep! She laughed hollowly as she marched up the stairs. She felt as limp as a wrung-out dishcloth and with the threat of losing her little boy hanging over her she doubted she would ever sleep again. But when she slid between the sheets her brain mercifully decided that it had had enough for one day, and her last thought was that she must set the alarm on the bedside clock.

Sergio woke to the sensation of his eyelids being prised open. After spending a hellish night on the most uncomfortable sofa he had ever encountered, he craved a couple of hours more sleep, especially when he glanced blearily at his watch and saw that it was five-thirty in the morning. He blinked and refocused on the angelic face hovering above him. Nico was staring at him with his big brown eyes framed by unbelievably long lashes. When he saw that Sergio was awake, he grinned.

'Daddy...'

Sergio felt his gut twist. 'Papà,' he said softly. 'I am your *papà*.' And you are *il mio bel ragazzo*. My beautiful boy, he thought to himself. Propping himself up on one elbow, he watched Nico line up his toy cars on the carpet. 'Is Mummy still asleep?'

Nico nodded. 'I got dressed,' he said proudly, patting his shorts.

That would explain why his T-shirt was on back to front, Sergio mused. He smiled. 'Clever boy.'

Nico lay on his stomach so that he could push his cars along the floor and Sergio suddenly froze. His eyes were drawn to the black bruises on the backs of the little boy's legs. Bile rose in his throat. *Santa Madre di Dio!* The marks were sickeningly familiar. When he had been a child, his legs had often been covered in bruises after a beating.

Swallowing hard, Sergio noticed another mark on Nico's body where his T-shirt had ridden up.

'Hey, little guy, let me turn your shirt around for you,' he murmured.

Nico obediently stood up and, as Sergio drew the shirt over his head, his breath hissed between his teeth at the sight of several more bruises on the child's ribs.

'How did you get hurt?' He somehow managed to keep his tone light.

'I was very naughty,' Nico told him with an innocence that tore Sergio's heart to shreds.

His head spun. He didn't know what was happening here. Everything inside him rejected the idea that Kristen could have inflicted the bruises on Nico. It was true she hadn't convinced him that she was an overly caring parent and he was deeply suspicious of her motive for finally deciding to tell him that he had a son, but it was hard to imagine that she would hurt her child.

But no one would ever have believed that his charming, beautiful mother had been capable of mental and physical cruelty, Sergio thought grimly. Patti had been the patron of a children's charity, but to her own child she had been a confusing figure—at times overly loving so that he had felt swamped, but she had been prone to violence when she had succumbed to her personal demon, alcohol, and at those times he had been afraid of her. He remembered the sick feeling in his stomach whenever she had summoned him to her study to be punished for the most minor misdemeanour. No one had heard his cries, and no one had come to his rescue—including his father.

Deep within Sergio's soul the scared, unhappy little boy he had once been took over his logical thought processes. A fundamental instinct to protect his child surged through him and he stood up and lifted Nico into his arms. 'How would you like to fly on an aeroplane, *piccolo*?' he murmured.

His heart turned over when Nico looked at him with his big, brown, *trusting* eyes. 'I will always protect you,' he promised his son gruffly, and was rewarded with a smile that somehow eased the loneliness that had haunted him since he had been a small boy who had longed to be with his own father.

CHAPTER SEVEN

WHEN KRISTEN OPENED her eyes she was puzzled to see a stream of bright sunlight filtering through the chink in the curtains. The house was quiet and, unusually, she was alone. Nico had a habit of climbing into her bed in the early hours and he would prod her awake and insist that she read him a story. He must still be asleep, she thought as she stretched, making the most of having the bed to herself.

She looked at the clock and her heart did a painful somersault. *It could not be half past nine!*

A frantic glance at her watch confirmed the worst. She leapt out of bed and cursed as she stubbed her toe on the bedside cabinet. Pulling on her dressing gown, she hurried along the hall and discovered that Nico's room was empty. It was unlike him to go downstairs on his own, but maybe he'd grown bored of waiting for her to wake up, she thought guiltily. Hell, she would have to phone Steph and apologise for being late for work for the second day in a row. With a dozen thoughts running around her head, Kristen pushed open the sitting room door and felt a flicker of unease when she saw that no one was there.

The blanket and pillow Sergio had used to make up a bed on the sofa were neatly folded, and Nico's toy cars were scattered across the carpet. Trying to control her panic, she continued into the kitchen. The half-drunk mug of coffee on the table indicated that Sergio must have left in a hurry. In the silence, the ticking of the clock seemed unnaturally loud. Fear cramped in Kristen's stomach. There had to be a reasonable explanation for Sergio and Nico's disappearance, she told herself.

Catching sight of the empty space where Nico's Wellington boots were kept by the back door, she felt weak with relief. Maybe Sergio had taken him for a walk or to the park.

The doorbell rang and she hurried to answer it, determined to impress on Sergio that he must not take Nico out without informing her first. But the man on the doorstep was a stranger—a short, swarthy man dressed in a suit, who introduced himself as Bernardo Valdi, Sergio's lawyer.

'Signor Castellano asked me to visit you.' The lawyer spoke in English but with a strong Italian accent. 'It might be better if we continue our discussion inside the house,' he added gently when Kristen gasped.

She stepped back to allow him to enter the hallway, suddenly finding that her legs felt like jelly. 'Where *is* Sergio? And, more importantly, where is my son?' she demanded in a trembling voice. Her fear returned, making her stomach churn as a terrible truth slowly dawned. 'He's taken him, hasn't he? Sergio has taken Nico.' Her voice rose. 'He won't get away with it. He has no right. I suppose he's gone back to the Hotel Royale. I'm going to call the police.'

'Calm yourself, *signorina*,' the lawyer said in a quietly authoritative voice. 'Signor Castellano has been granted an emergency custody order of his son.'

'Emergency…' Kristen stared at the lawyer dazedly, wondering, hoping that this was all a horrible nightmare. 'On what grounds?' she whispered.

'The *signor* was concerned for the child's welfare after he saw bruises on him.'

'Dear God! He thinks I hurt Nico?' Nausea threatened to overwhelm her. 'I have to see Sergio and explain.' She stumbled down the hall. 'I'll get dressed and go straight to the hotel.'

'They are not there, *signorina*. Signor Castellano flew to Sicily on his private jet an hour ago, and he has taken his son with him.' Bernardo Valdi gave an exclamation as he reached Kristen's side just in time to catch her as her knees sagged.

The taxi had turned off the main highway running from the airport at Catania to the coastal town of Taormina, and was now heading along narrow roads leading to the Castellano estate. Kristen stared out of the window at the breathtaking Sicilian countryside and felt an ache in her heart. Everywhere was unchanged and familiar, as if time had stood still for the past four years. Farmhouses and small villages dotted the landscape. In early summer the fields were still green but would turn to gold as the crops ripened, and on the far horizon Mount Etna's peak still wore a snowy mantle. The great volcano was sleeping today and only a thin stream of white smoke drifted from its summit into the blue sky.

As they passed a vast olive grove, Kristen's tension increased. She recognised the area and knew that the gates of the Castellano estate were around the next bend. She also knew that the gatehouse was manned by security guards twenty-four hours a day and visitors were strictly vetted before being allowed to enter.

Bernardo Valdi's visit had left her distraught and utterly determined to find her son. It had been easy enough to book a seat on the first available flight to Sicily, but as the taxi drew nearer to the estate she had no plan of action in the likely event that Sergio would refuse to allow her to see Nico. Her nerves jangled as the taxi stopped in front of a set of huge iron gates and a security guard approached. She fully expected to be turned away when the guard spoke on his mobile phone and relayed her name to someone at the house but, to her surprise and relief, he stepped back and waved the car through the electronic gates as they swung open.

The gravel driveway continued for a quarter of a mile before it forked into three separate roads. One led to the main house, La Casa Bianca, where Kristen assumed Sergio's father Tito still lived. Another road disappeared into a pine forest, and in the distance the turrets of a castle—which had been built in the thirteenth century by a Sicilian nobleman and ancestor of the current Castellano family—were just visible above the tree tops. Four years ago, Sergio's brother Salvatore and his beautiful wife Adriana had lived at the castle with their daughter, Kristen recalled.

The taxi took the third road, which wound through an orange grove and skirted a turquoise lake before the terracotta-coloured walls of a large, elegant villa came into view. Casa Camelia held so many memories. Her mind flew back to the first time Sergio had invited her to his home. They had eaten dinner on the terrace overlooking the garden and later he had carried her upstairs to his bedroom and made love to her. It had been her first time, and she had sensed that Sergio had been shocked when he'd discovered she was a virgin. But he had been so gentle, Kristen remembered. The pain of his possession had been fleeting, and the pleasure that had come afterwards when he had brought her to orgasm with his skill and patience had taken her heart prisoner.

How could their relationship have gone so spectacularly wrong that they were now enemies fighting over their son? she thought emotionally. The simple answer was that Sergio had not loved her, while she had loved him too much. She had left him before he could break her heart, but she had been too late.

The taxi drew up in front of the villa and Kristen dismissed her memories of the past as she focused on the battle she knew she faced to reclaim her little boy. Her heart slammed against her ribs as she ran up the stone steps. Someone must have watched her arrive because the front door opened and an elderly man wearing a butler's uniform ushered her inside. A lightning glance around the large entrance hall revealed that it had not changed since she had last been there. The white walls reflected the sunlight streaming through the mullioned windows and sunbeams danced across the black marble floor.

Kristen's eyes flew to the two men standing in the hall. Sergio and his twin brother were strikingly similar in appearance, but she noted with a flare of shock that Salvatore Castellano had changed dramatically since she had last seen him. His once-handsome face was thinner, almost haggard, and his mouth was set in a stern line as if he had not smiled for a long time. His black hair fell to his shoulders and was as unkempt as the stubble that shaded his jaw, and his eyes were dull and hard as lava spewed from Etna that had solidified into black rock.

Salvatore walked towards her with a pronounced limp, and Kristen wondered what had happened to him. 'Kristen, it's good to see you again,' he murmured. Like Sergio, his hard features rarely showed any emotion and she had no idea if he was surprised by her visit. He headed out of the front door, but Kristen was barely aware of him leaving as she stared at Sergio.

Dressed in beige chinos and a cream shirt that contrasted with his olive skin, he looked gorgeous and so relaxed that Kristen's tenuous hold on her composure snapped. How dared he appear as if he did not have a care in the world when she had just spent the worst few hours of her life? Anger swept through her. She resented his powerful physical presence and resented even more her fierce sexual awareness of him.

'Where is Nico? I was so worried when I woke up and found you had gone. When your lawyer said you had taken him…' Her voice cracked as she relived the sheer terror she had felt when she'd feared she might never see Nico again.

Suddenly she was crying, great tearing sobs that wracked her slender frame. 'You bastard!' she choked. Tears streamed down her face, and the need to hurt him as much as he had hurt her made her lift her hand and connect it sharply with his cheek. The sound of the slap echoed around the vast hall and the moment she had done it she felt sick. Physical violence was completely alien to her, yet twice in two days she had lashed out at Sergio. How could she blame him for believing that she was responsible for the terrible bruises on Nico's legs after the way she had behaved?

Sergio had not reacted to the slap, even though he could easily have grabbed her wrist and prevented her from striking him. His expression was unreadable, but for an instant some indefinable emotion flared in his eyes as he watched her fall apart.

Kristen could not stop crying. It was as if a dam had burst inside her, and as she dashed her tears away more came in an unstoppable river. 'I didn't hurt Nico, I swear. I would never lay a finger on him. He fell from the top of the climbing frame at the park. I had told him not to climb too high, but he's such a daredevil and sometimes he can be quite naughty and disobedient. When he slipped I was scared he would hit the ground and break every bone in his body.' She shuddered at the memory of Nico's scream as he had plummeted from the climbing frame. 'Thankfully, I managed to catch him, but during the fall he slammed against the metal bars and was bruised all over his body and legs.'

Recalling the terrifying incident, Kristen couldn't regain control of her emotions. Her chest heaved and she searched desperately in her handbag for a tissue. 'How could you think I would have inflicted those bruises on him? I'm not a bad mother. I love Nico with all my heart and I would never harm him.'

Sergio studied Kristen dispassionately. Her face was blotchy and tear-stained and her eyes were red-rimmed. She had obviously dressed in a hurry and not checked her appearance in a mirror, because if she had she would have seen that her orange T-shirt and pink cardigan clashed horribly. Continuing his inspection, he glanced down and saw that she was wearing mismatched shoes—on one foot a navy blue trainer and on the other a white plimsoll.

Following his gaze, she flushed. 'I left the house in a rush. Which is understandable when you had snatched my son,' she added defensively.

She must have been frantic about Nico not to have noticed that she had put on odd shoes!

As Sergio watched Kristen scrub her hand over her wet face the tight knot of tension in his gut slowly unravelled. The doctor who he had called to the villa to check over Nico had said that the bruises on his legs were probably the result of an accident, and in his opinion were not signs that he had been mistreated. Kristen's explanation about Nico falling from the climbing frame was believable. Her distress was real and painful to witness, he acknowledged uncomfortably. Was it possible he had misjudged her? Doubt crept into Sergio's mind. When he had seen the bruises on Nico his emotions had taken over from his usual cool logic and he had been tormented by memories of how his mother had treated him when he had been a child. His only thought had been to rescue Nico and bring him to Sicily. But perhaps he had overreacted?

'Kristen, you have to stop crying,' he said roughly. 'Nico is ill and he needs you.'

Her eyes widened. 'What's wrong with him?'

'He's running a high temperature and he's been sick. The doctor thinks he has picked up a gastric virus.'

'There's been a vomiting bug going around at nursery.' Kristen drew a ragged breath and finally managed to stop crying. She knew she did not cry prettily and she probably looked a mess, she thought ruefully. But the news that Nico was unwell drove all other considerations from her mind. 'Where is he? Why aren't you with him?'

'The nanny who looks after Salvatore's daughter has been helping to care for him. I'll take you straight to him. Did you ask the taxi driver to bring in your luggage?'

'I don't have any luggage. I'm not planning on staying. I'm here to collect Nico and take him home.'

Sergio's eyes narrowed on her determined face and he seemed about to argue, but thought better of it. 'We will discuss what is best for him later. You certainly won't be taking him anywhere while he's throwing up.'

Kristen hurried after Sergio up the sweeping staircase. On the first-floor landing they walked past the master bedroom. The door was open and she could not resist peeping in. The wallpaper and soft furnishings had been updated and were a soft blue rather than gold as she remembered, but the huge four-poster bed still dominated the room and the sight of it evoked memories she wished she could forget. Now was not a good time to recall in vivid detail

Sergio's naked, muscular body, or to remember the fire-storm passion they had once shared and his unexpected tenderness when he made love to her.

There was no hint of tenderness about him now, she noted as she caught up with him. He was waiting outside the door next to his room. His unreadable expression became speculative when his glance travelled from her flushed face to his bedroom but he made no comment other than to say, 'Nico has been asking for you.'

'I'm not surprised. He was probably frightened when you whisked him away from everything that is familiar to him and brought him to a place he has never seen before. What were you thinking of?' Kristen asked him curtly. 'You told me that when you were a young child your mother snatched you and took you to another country. How could you do the same thing to Nico?'

His jaw tightened. 'I had my reasons.'

'Or maybe you were trying to score a point over me and prove how powerful you are?' she said cynically. 'This isn't one of your boardroom battles.' Kristen broke off at the sound of Nico crying. Her fight with Sergio could wait until later.

Pushing open the door, she entered an elegant bedroom which had a pale carpet and silk covers on the bed that were hardly suitable for a pre-school child, especially one with a stomach upset. Nico looked feverish; his cheeks were flushed and his curls clustered damply on his brow. A woman was leaning over him, trying to persuade him to take a sip of water, but he pushed her away and his sobs grew louder until he looked across the room and saw Kristen.

'*Mummy...*' His lip quivered, and his distress tore Kristen's heart. She dashed over to the bed and gathered him in her arms.

'It's all right, sweetheart. I'm here.' She frowned at Sergio. 'He feels very hot. Have you given him anything to bring his temperature down?'

'He brought up the medicine the doctor left for him,' Sergio started to explain, but at that moment Nico was sick again—all over Kristen. '*Santa Madre!* I can't believe he's got anything left in his stomach,' Sergio muttered as he sprang forward to lift the little boy off her lap. But Nico clung to her and wouldn't let go.

'Leave him,' Kristen said quietly. 'I'll get cleaned up later.'

'But you're covered…'

'It doesn't matter. Pass me a towel so that I can mop him up.' She gave Sergio a fierce look. 'This is what parenting is. It's not about buying expensive toys—it's about being there for your child when he needs you.' She glanced towards the woman who she guessed was the nanny Sergio had mentioned. 'Please leave me alone with him. He's confused and upset, and having people around him that he doesn't know isn't helping.'

It was the early hours of the following morning before Nico showed signs that the worst of the vomiting virus was over. His temperature dropped back to normal and he fell into a comfortable sleep.

'He'll probably be absolutely fine and full of energy when he wakes up,' Kristen told Sergio, who had remained to help nurse the little boy, although he had sent the nanny away. She tucked the sheet around Nico and moved away from the bed so that her voice did not disturb him. 'You'll be amazed at how resilient children are.' As she spoke she was hit by a wave of exhaustion and collapsed onto the sofa.

'He already looks a whole lot better than you do,' Sergio

murmured drily, comparing Nico's healthy colour with Kristen's white face. He quickly looked away from her, unable to meet her gaze. During the past few hours she had proved beyond doubt her devotion to her son. Her patience as she had attended to Nico when he had been sick and comforted him with loving care had shown Sergio how wrong he had been about her, and he felt guilty that he had misjudged her so badly. She was nothing like his mother, thank God. He knew he owed her an explanation of why he had snatched Nico, but he did not find it easy to talk about his childhood experiences.

He sat down next to her on the sofa and felt her instantly become tense. Was she afraid of him? He couldn't blame her after the way he had behaved, he thought grimly. The worry he had put her through when he had disappeared with Nico was evident in her drawn features. She looked infinitely fragile, and when he brushed a stray tendril of hair back from her cheek she jerked away from him as if he had struck her.

But it was not fear he saw in her eyes, although her expression was wary and mistrustful. He deserved that, Sergio accepted. He had done nothing to earn her trust. What he found more intriguing was the fact that her pupils had dilated and her chest was rising and falling unevenly. Sexual awareness could not be denied or disguised, however hard she might try to hide her feelings. His analytical brain acknowledged that her attraction to him was the ace up his sleeve. The first rule of business was to discover your opponent's weakness, and it was useful to know that Kristen was vulnerable where he was concerned.

'Why do you and Nico have the surname Lloyd?' he asked her. 'When I knew you four years ago your name was Russell, so why did you change it?' His jaw tightened as an unwelcome thought occurred to him. 'Did you marry some guy who then became a stepfather to Nico?'

'No, of course not. There hasn't been anyone…' She broke off abruptly, making Sergio wonder if she had been about to say that she had not dated anyone since him. He hoped that was the case, but only because he hated the idea that she might have introduced a boyfriend to Nico, not because the thought of her having sex with another guy made his insides burn as if he had swallowed acid, he assured himself.

'Russell was my stepfather's name,' Kristen explained. 'My real father, David Lloyd, died when I was a baby. When I was eight my mother married my gymnastics coach, Alan Russell, and I took his name.'

'I remember your stepfather. He made it clear that he did not approve of me.' Sergio frowned. 'I only met him once when I came to see you at your rented villa, and he warned me to stay away from you.'

'He didn't approve of anything that distracted me from my training. And you were a major distraction.' Kristen sighed. 'Four years ago I came to Sicily with my mum and Alan, but they were called home and while they were in England I met you. When Alan came back to Sicily he was furious when he discovered I was having an affair with you instead of focusing on my gymnastics training.

'While I was growing up I was very close to Alan. He was a top coach and he spotted my potential early on. It was his dream as much as mine that I should become a champion gymnast. Sometimes…' she hesitated '…I've wondered if he married Mum so that he could have control over me and my career. He was a very domineering man, but the attention he gave me made me feel special and I wanted to do well and please him. But as I grew older I started to resent the fact that I had no other life outside of gymnastics. Alan insisted I followed a rigorous training schedule and I never had time for anything else, including boyfriends.'

'I discovered just how innocent you were,' Sergio said drily. 'Why didn't you tell me you were a virgin?'

Kristen blushed. 'I was scared you wouldn't make love to me if you knew it was my first time…and I desperately wanted you to,' she admitted.

He gave a harsh laugh. 'You were not the only desperate one, *cara*. I'd like to think that if I had known of your innocence I would have held back, but the truth is I wanted you so badly that I could not resist you.'

The possessive gleam in his eyes sent a quiver through Kristen. She recognised the sexual chemistry between them was as intense as it had been four years ago, but her instincts told her to fight the damnable desire that made her body tremble. He had hurt her once before, and she must not forget his threat that he wanted to take Nico from her.

'What was your mother and stepfather's reaction when you told them you were pregnant?'

'Mum was fine about it. But Alan was furious. He knew that if I had a baby it would probably end my gymnastics career. He pushed me hard because my achievements at competitions enhanced his reputation as a top coach, but I suppose I'd always believed that he actually cared about me as a person.' She swallowed. 'He had been my dad since I was eight and I…I loved him. But he tried to persuade me to have an abortion and, when I refused, he threw me out and wouldn't even let me stay at home until after the baby had been born.'

Her stepfather's rejection, coming on top of what she had taken as Sergio's rejection when she had lost Nico's twin and she had felt that he had not wanted their baby, had had a deep impact on Kristen. She had felt betrayed and abandoned by the two men she loved. Both had only been interested in what she could give them; Alan had lavished attention on her because he had hoped she would win sporting glory and enhance his coaching reputation, and Sergio had wanted her for sex. Four years on, the hurt hadn't faded, and she wondered if she could ever trust a man again. She had developed a fierce sense of independence. As a single mother totally responsible for her son, she could not afford to let her guard down.

She forced her mind from the past as Sergio said harshly, 'You mean you were homeless when you had Nico but you still did not tell me you had given birth to my child? *Dio*, did you hate me so much that you preferred to struggle alone rather than come to me for help?'

'I didn't hate you. But when I left Sicily our relationship was over. I've explained that because of what you said at the hospital I believed you would not have been interested in my pregnancy. I lived in my student digs until just before Nico was born, and on my twenty-first birthday I inherited some money from my real father which I used for a deposit to buy a house. That's when I changed my name back from Russell to Lloyd.' Kristen had wanted to end all links with her stepfather. 'I had to work full-time to pay the mortgage. Alan had thrown Mum out too because she supported my decision to have the baby, which made me wonder if he had ever truly loved her,' she said heavily. 'Anyway, Mum moved in with me and she looked after Nico during the day.

'He has only been going to day care for a few months, since…' she swallowed '…since Mum was killed in an accident. That's why he hasn't settled at nursery. He misses his nana. And that is why I decided to tell you about him. I wanted to be a full-time mum to Nico for a few months.

But I couldn't afford not to work and so I was going to ask you for financial help, just temporarily.'

The tremor in Kristen's voice had a profound effect on Sergio. 'I'm sorry about your mother. I remember you were very close to her.'

'Yeah,' Kristen said gruffly. His gentleness was unexpected and she quickly looked away from him, willing herself not to cry. 'It's Nico I'm worried about. I want to do what's best for him.'

'And you have,' Sergio assured her. 'I'm glad you came to me for help, and I'm glad that you are both here at Casa Camelia.'

'You didn't leave me much choice after you brought Nico here without my consent.' Kristen shot him a sharp look. 'As soon as he is better I want to take him home.'

'This is his home.' He met her gaze levelly and although he spoke quietly Kristen heard the implacable determination in his voice, which filled her with despair.

'You saw tonight how much he needs me,' she said urgently.

'I agree. But our son deserves to grow up with his father as well as his mother.'

For most of his childhood, after his mother had taken him to America, Sergio had longed to be with his father. But for ten years he'd had no contact with Tito and when they had finally met again it had been too late to establish the bond that should exist between a father and his son. *A bond that Sergio was determined to forge with his own son.*

Somehow he needed to convince Kristen that Nico would benefit from growing up with his father. But she mistrusted him, and he was beginning to understand how deeply she had been affected by the way he had responded when she had miscarried Nico's twin. He had tried to reassure her that the miscarriage had in no way been her fault, but she had misunderstood his words and thought that he had not wanted their child. It was little wonder that she had kept Nico a secret, Sergio thought grimly. She was a fantastic mother, but it was obvious that she had been struggling to bring Nico up on her own, and the truth was the little boy needed both his parents.

Fear cramped in Kristen's stomach. 'So you still intend to fight for custody of him?'

'I hope we can come to an arrangement by which we can both be involved in Nico's upbringing. You told me you wanted to take a break from work to spend time with him,' Sergio reminded her. 'What I am suggesting is that you and Nico stay here at Casa Camelia for a few weeks while we discuss his future.'

'And if I don't want to stay?'

His eyes met hers, and for a split second Kristen thought she saw a plea for understanding in his gaze. But she heard the determination in his voice when he said, 'You are not a prisoner, *cara*. You can leave whenever you like—but Nico will remain here with me.'

CHAPTER EIGHT

THE WARM, SCENTED bath water was having a soporific effect on Kristen. Her eyelids felt as though they were weighted down and she was having trouble keeping them open. Would Sergio find it convenient if she drowned in his bath? she wondered. It would mean he would gain custody of Nico without a court battle.

The thought of Nico being motherless made her haul herself upright. She would fight to her last breath to stay with him, but there was no escaping the fact that Sergio had the upper hand now that he had brought Nico to Sicily. He had told her she was not his prisoner, but she was trapped at Casa Camelia by her love for her son.

She was too tired to think any more. When Sergio had offered to run her a bath she had agreed without argument, especially when he had remarked in an amused voice that she didn't smell too good after Nico had been sick on her. At least her hair was now clean and rather more fragrant, and when she stepped out of the bath she discovered that Sergio had left one of his shirts for her to wear.

After blasting her hair with a drier, she emerged from the en suite bathroom and was relieved to find he was not in his bedroom. On her way out of the room she noticed a photograph of a beautiful raven-haired woman on the desk, and her heart gave a lurch when she recognised it was

the woman she had seen four years ago in a magazine—
Sergio's first wife, who he had loved but was now dead.
She studied the photo. For so long she had felt jealous of
the woman Sergio had married, but now she felt sad for
her. She must have been tragically young when she had
died. Her mind reeling with confused thoughts, Kristen
walked through the connecting door into the adjoining
bedroom where Nico was sleeping soundly.

He looked angelic with his dark curls spread on the
white pillow, and his cheeks had lost their feverish flush
and were a healthy pink. He was cuddling Hippo. Thank
goodness Sergio had remembered to bring his favourite
toy.

He would be a good father. The thought slid into her
head, and she bit her lip as she remembered how gentle he
had been with Nico when he had been ill. Sergio had stated
that their son deserved to grow up with both his parents
and she was finding it hard to disagree, but her life was
in London and he based himself in Sicily and travelled
around the world for his job.

How could they share custody of Nico and give him the
stable and secure upbringing that every child needed? She
certainly wouldn't allow him to be passed between them
like a parcel, Kristen thought fiercely. The future suddenly
seemed frighteningly uncertain. Maybe things would be
clearer after a few hours' sleep. It was four o'clock in the
morning and after the tension of the last few days she was
bone-weary, she acknowledged as she curled up on the bed.

When Sergio walked into the room fifteen minutes later
he found Kristen fast asleep, one arm draped protectively
across Nico. The sight of mother and child snuggled up
together brought a lump to his throat. He couldn't remember Patti ever showing him affection, and he was fiercely
glad that his son had a mother who clearly adored him.

But he loved Nico too. His son had captured his heart instantly. How could he not love his own flesh and blood, the gorgeous little boy whose angelic looks were enhanced by his impish smile? How could his own mother not have loved *him*? Sergio wondered bleakly. Had there been something about him that had made him unlovable? Was that the reason his father had not tried harder to regain custody of him?

Nico would never have reason to doubt that his parents loved him, Sergio vowed. He accepted that Kristen had believed she'd had good reasons for choosing to bring up Nico on her own, but he was determined to convince her that cooperation between them would be far better for their son than a custody battle. When they had met at the Hotel Royale he had known he wanted to resume their affair, but now the stakes were higher.

Four years ago he had guessed that she had been in love with him and, although he had no expectation that she still was, he was convinced that she had not slept with him the other night simply because the sex was good. More than good, he amended. She was the only woman who had ever made him lose control. During their affair he had fought the feelings she stirred in him, but now the only battle he planned to fight with Kristen was to persuade her to allow him to have a presence in her life as well as Nico's. And, for Sergio, losing was not an option.

Kristen rolled over on the mattress and came into contact with something warm and solid. Her brain fuzzily realised that the object was too hard to be a pillow and too large to be Nico, and when she opened her eyes her first thought was that she was not in the room where she had fallen asleep. She turned her head and her heart practically leapt out of her chest.

'What are you doing in my bed?' she demanded, uncaring that Sergio appeared to be asleep.

He opened his eyes and gave her a lazy, sexy smile that did nothing to help slow her racing pulse. 'Actually, you are in my bed.'

'Not from choice,' she assured him grittily. His amused expression fuelled her temper and she welcomed her anger as a much-needed distraction from her awareness of his virile body. The disturbing thought struck her that he could very well be naked beneath the sheet draped across his hips. And not only naked! Her gaze slid down his body and the sight of his obvious arousal straining against the silk sheet made her catch her breath.

She needed to take control of the situation. Folding her arms across her chest made her feel more authoritative and hid her pebble-hard nipples. 'How did I get here?'

'I brought you to my room because I heard you crying in your sleep and I didn't want you to disturb Nico. You spoke your mother's name,' Sergio added gently.

She swallowed. 'I dream about her sometimes.' She looked away from him, feeling incredibly vulnerable. She had a vague recollection of being upset and feeling comforted by strong arms that had held her. Another memory, of running her hands over a broad, hair-roughened chest made her blush and hope fervently that it had all been part of a dream.

'I was glad I was able to comfort you.' Sergio confirmed the worst and Kristen winced with embarrassment to know that she had actually stroked her hands over him while she had been asleep.

'I'm sorry if I disturbed you,' she said stiffly.

'Having your gorgeous body cuddled up close to me was no hardship, *cara*.'

Beneath his softly teasing tone, Kristen heard something deeper and darker that evoked a coiling sensation in the pit of her stomach. Desire throbbed between them, but she could not, would not fall into its delicious embrace.

Panic sharpened her voice. 'I did not cuddle up to you.'

'Oh yes, you did.' He moved so fast that before she had realised what was happening she was lying flat on her back and his hard body was covering hers so that she could feel every muscle and sinew of his thighs pressed against her. Even more shocking was the feel of his rock-solid arousal jabbing into her belly, and she couldn't prevent her body's instinctive response as molten heat pooled between her legs.

'You clung to me like a limpet,' he taunted. 'And you cried out my name. Perhaps returning to Casa Camelia brought back memories of all that we shared four years ago?'

'All we *shared* was sex.' Somehow Kristen managed to sound scathing; refusing to let him see how much his words affected her. She pushed against his chest and tried to slide out from beneath him, but he had pinned her to the bed and every slight movement she made resulted in his burgeoning arousal nudging deeper between her thighs. 'You didn't share anything else with me, least of all yourself. You kept a barrier between us and I never knew what you were thinking…or feeling.'

'I gave you more than I've ever given to any other woman,' he told her intently.

'Am I supposed to feel flattered by that? Was I supposed to feel grateful that you fitted me into your busy work schedule?'

'I asked you to stay in Sicily with me. You were the one who chose to leave.'

'Because I knew that if I had stayed as your mistress our relationship would have been all on your terms. You expected me to give up everything that was important to me, even though you knew that gymnastics was a big part of my life.'

'My position as head of a division of the Castellano Group necessitated me travelling extensively and working long hours. But you needed to be in England to train with the gymnastics team. I couldn't see how we could continue our affair if we were rarely together or even in the same country.' Sergio exhaled heavily. 'The reason my parents divorced was because my mother was determined to pursue an acting career in America and she and my father never spent any time together.'

'We could have tried to work something out. But you refused to make compromises. You made me feel that I was unimportant and that my feelings didn't count.' Kristen bit her lip. 'You did the same at the hotel in London. You were in such a hurry to have sex that we still had our clothes on, and as soon as it was over you were on your phone, no doubt discussing business. You made me feel cheap,' she muttered.

'I answered the call because I knew it was from my brother. He is the only person who has the number of my private phone so that he can contact me if there is a problem with our father. Tito's health is not good, and Salvatore rang to tell me he was unwell. I would have explained why I had left you so abruptly…but you had already gone.'

Sergio smoothed her hair back from her brow and looked deeply into her eyes. 'I'm sorry you felt that I did not show you the proper respect you deserve. It's no excuse that my impatience was because I was desperate to make love to you, but I had hoped you would spend the night with me and I intended to act with a little more finesse the next time we had sex.' He shifted his position so that his pelvis ground against Kristen's, and she caught her breath as he whispered in her ear, 'But, instead of telling you what I'd planned, let me demonstrate.'

'I don't need you to demonstrate anything.' She gritted her teeth as she fought the insidious heat of sexual longing that surged through her veins. 'Let me go, Sergio. I need to check on Nico.'

'I went to see him just before you woke up. He's sound asleep, and I have asked the nanny, Luisa, to sit with him while you get some rest.'

She swallowed as he began to undo the buttons running down the front of the shirt she had worn to sleep in. 'Why are you doing this?' she asked desperately. 'What we had was over a long time ago.'

'Was it, Krissie?' He worked his way down the shirt until he reached the last button. 'Can you honestly say that you never thought of me in the last four years, that you never lay awake at night, remembering the touch of my hands on your skin?'

His glittering gaze held her captive as he spread the shirt open and curled his hands possessively around her breasts. 'I remember everything. Making love to you again at the hotel reminded me of just how good it was between us, and now that you have come back into my life I am in no hurry to let you go.'

There were a hundred reasons why she should not allow herself to be seduced by Sergio's velvet-soft voice and the sensual promise in his eyes. She would be mad to respond to the brush of his lips across hers. But her willpower had always been non-existent where he was concerned, Kristen acknowledged dismally. She had spent too many nights tormented by memories of him and her resistance was melting faster than candle wax in a flame as he skimmed his hands over her naked body, making her skin tingle everywhere he touched.

Her heart leapt when he teased her lips apart with his tongue and when he kissed her, slow and sweet, as if he had missed her as much as she had missed him, she responded to him helplessly, her misgivings swept away by the tidal wave of desire that obliterated all rational thought.

Their previous encounter at the hotel had been fast and frantic, but now Sergio took his time to explore her body and rediscover the pleasure points that made her tremble and gasp when he caressed her.

'I love that your breasts are so sensitive,' he murmured as he flicked his tongue over one rosy peak and then its twin until they hardened. He closed his mouth around her nipple and sucked until she whimpered with pleasure.

Sergio still knew her body so well, even though it was so long since they had been in a relationship. Kristen felt a sharp stab of jealousy that he must have made love to other women in the last four years. Don't think, her brain urged, just feel. She was no longer the naïve girl who had fallen in love with him. She understood that her desire for him was just sexual chemistry, and after four years of celibacy it was not surprising that she was impatient to experience the pleasure of his possession.

Her stomach muscles contracted when he trailed his fingertips over her abdomen and explored the dip of her navel, before moving lower. He eased his hand beneath her knickers and slowly, so slowly that she wanted to scream, he inched towards the place where she was desperate for him to touch her. She was embarrassingly wet so that when he gently parted her and slid his fingers between her silken folds her body accepted him willingly and her excitement increased as he teased her clitoris until she gasped and tensed.

'Not yet, *cara*,' he murmured against her mouth before he kissed her deeply. 'This time I promised we would take things slowly.' This time Sergio wanted her to be reassured that he was not seeking quick satisfaction. She had accused him of withholding himself from her during their affair, and he acknowledged the truth of that. His habit of keeping his emotions locked away was too deeply ingrained, but at least he could show her how much he desired her.

His heart kicked in his chest as he pulled her panties off and she spread her legs invitingly. He found her eagerness touching and the realisation that she wanted him as badly as he wanted her gave him hope that he had not lost her. It took all his willpower not to plunge his painfully hard erection into her slick heat, but he resisted the ache in his gut and lowered his head to inhale the sweet scent of her arousal.

Kristen gave a startled gasp when Sergio ran his tongue up and down her moist opening, parting her so that he could bestow the most intimate caress of all. She knew he was fiercely aroused and she had assumed he was impatient to satisfy his own needs, but he was showing her with his clever fingers and wickedly invasive tongue that he was focused entirely on giving her pleasure.

He had a magician's skill, she thought dazedly. Her limbs trembled as he took her to the edge and held her there. The dedication he applied to arousing her made her feel cherished, and when he claimed her mouth once more and kissed her with tenderness as well as passion she knew with an ache in her heart that she was slipping under his spell and there was nothing she could do about it.

Her breath caught in her throat as he positioned himself over her and deftly donned a protective sheath. His golden-skinned body gleamed like satin and the faint abrasion of his chest hairs against her breasts was intensely erotic. Memories of the many times he had made love to her in this room, in this bed, danced through her mind and it seemed the most natural thing in the world to lift her hips towards him as he plunged forward and drove his powerful arousal deep inside her.

'Krissie…' His voice shook, as if he recognised that the connection between them was more than the physical joining of their bodies. But as he began to move, thrusting into her with strong, measured strokes, Kristen stopped thinking and her sensory perception took over. She could hear her blood thundering in her ears, echoing the ragged sound of his quickened breathing. Faster, faster, every devastating thrust increased her excitement. She clung to his sweat-slicked shoulders while he rode her, possessed her, and just when she was sure she could not take any more, he tipped her over the edge and into the most intense orgasm of her life.

'Open your eyes.' Sergio's voice was rough and when Kristen obeyed his command she was startled by the blazing intensity of his gaze. 'I want you to know that it's me you're making love with, me who is giving you pleasure— not some other lover.' Jealousy was a new emotion to him and it burned like acid in his gut.

'I haven't had any other lovers.' She knew as she said the words that she had revealed too much of herself, but strangely she did not care that she had made herself even more vulnerable. She could not lie, and she was glad she had been truthful when he breathed her name like a prayer and kissed her mouth with aching sweetness.

'Tesoro…' Sergio's iron control finally snapped and he climaxed violently, his head thrown back and his throat moving convulsively as he pumped his seed into her and his big body shuddered.

In the aftermath of their passion he lay on top of her, his dark head resting on her breasts. Kristen's heartbeat gradually slowed and she became conscious of her surroundings once more. The bright sunlight streaming through the slatted blinds made her realise that she had no idea of the time. Her frantic journey to Sicily and the hours that she had spent taking care of Nico while he had been ill had played havoc with her body clock.

The strident peal of the phone was an unwelcome intrusion, and as Sergio rolled off her and answered it she was hit by a cold blast of reality. Nothing had changed. They had had mind-blowing sex, but now it was business as usual. His commitment to the Castellano Group was total, and he had probably already forgotten her and was focused on the next big deal.

To her surprise, he cut the call after a brief conversation in Italian. 'That was Luisa, to say that Nico is awake.'

Nico! Guilt swept through Kristen that she had forgotten about him while she had been in Sergio's bed. It was ridiculous to feel shy with Sergio after she had made love with him but she couldn't meet his gaze as she slid out of bed and quickly pulled on the shirt he had lent her, wincing as the material grazed her sensitised nipples.

'I must go to him,' she muttered. 'I hope he hasn't been sick again.'

'Luisa assured me that he woke up full of beans, ate all his breakfast and now he's playing with his train set. But I agree we ought to get up. We're due to have lunch with my father in an hour, which means, regrettably, that we can't spend the rest of the day in bed like we used to do.' Sergio studied her pink cheeks speculatively. 'Do you remember, *cara*, how sometimes we would make love for hours and only leave the bedroom when we needed food?'

'Four years is a long time, and I don't remember much about our affair,' Kristen lied. Anxious to change the subject, she asked, 'Do you know what happened to my clothes?'

'The maid took them to be washed after Nico was sick over you. But in the wardrobe you will find a few outfits that I ordered for you from a friend who owns a boutique in Palermo.'

'A few outfits' turned out to be a whole range of clothes, from formal evening dresses to casual-wear that bore designer labels, which Kristen knew were completely out of her price range. 'I don't need all these clothes, and I can't afford them,' she said as she flicked through the rail. 'You suggested that Nico and I should stay here for a couple of weeks so that he can have a holiday, but I'll have to go back to my job in London…and I'll be taking him with me.'

'We have a lot to discuss,' Sergio said non-committally. 'Perhaps you can solve a puzzle for me. I sent a member of my staff to your house in Camden to bring back some of your clothes, but all Marco could find were a few items that look frankly as though they belong in a charity shop.'

Kristen shrugged. 'That's where I buy most of my clothes. You can find some real bargains if you look carefully.'

'I'll take your word for it. But if you buy second-hand clothes, why do you have thousands of pounds' worth of credit card debts and bills for designer goods?'

Realising that she had no option but to tell him the truth, she sighed heavily. 'I'm not in debt…but Mum owed a fortune when she died. The letters you saw from debt collecting agencies are trying to claim money from her estate. But Mum only had a few hundred pounds in savings, and that has already gone to her creditors.

'Don't think badly of her,' she told Sergio fiercely, even though he'd not said a word. 'I had no idea that she was so unhappy being married to my stepfather. She admitted that she only stayed with Alan because he was my gymnastics coach and she didn't want to ruin my chances of success.

But he was a very controlling man and he destroyed her confidence. She used to go shopping to make herself feel better, but it became a compulsion. It was a form of depression. She never even wore the things she bought; she just hid them at the back of the wardrobe.

'When Alan found out that she had run up huge debts he refused to help her sort things out. The worry of it made her ill, and so I took charge of her finances and I've been trying to repay the money she owed. Even after Mum died, the debt agencies have still been hounding me.'

She glanced at Sergio, wishing she knew what he was thinking, but his expression gave nothing away.

'Your mother was lucky to have such a loyal daughter,' he said gently.

Kristen bit her lip. 'She sacrificed her happiness for me and my gymnastics career. My stepfather always demanded his own way. Who does that remind me of?' she said sarcastically. 'You snatched Nico and brought him to Sicily because it was what you wanted.'

'I acted in his best interests.' Even though he had been wrong to think that Kristen had been responsible for the bruises on Nico, Sergio still believed it was better for the little boy to be in Sicily rather than living in a tiny, shabby house in Camden and spending all day at nursery. Somehow he had to convince Kristen of that.

He threw back the sheet and gave her a sardonic look when she blushed at the sight of his naked body. 'If you keep staring at me like you're doing, we definitely won't make it to lunch,' he drawled.

But, although her flush deepened at his taunt, she kept her eyes fixed on him as he strolled across the room. Her desire for him was his secret weapon and he had no compunction about using it mercilessly, Sergio thought. Sex was the one way he could connect with her and he slid his hand beneath her chin and slanted his mouth over hers to kiss her with passion and a possessiveness that he had never felt for any other woman.

Her response tested his resolve and he felt a pang of regret when he eventually ended the kiss and traced his thumb over her swollen bottom lip. 'My father is looking forward to meeting his grandson,' he said roughly, 'so I'd better leave you to get dressed.'

CHAPTER NINE

NICO WAS WEARING a new pair of jeans and a T-shirt and looked the picture of health when Sergio lifted him into the car. Kristen was relieved that he had completely recovered from the vomiting virus. He seemed to have settled into his new surroundings at Casa Camelia, but she was not sure whether it was a good thing. She didn't want him to be upset when she took him back home to London. Sergio had said that Sicily was Nico's home and perhaps a judge would agree and award custody of him to his father, she thought worriedly.

With Nico safely strapped into the child seat in the rear of the car, Sergio slid into the driver's seat and Kristen felt her stomach dip as her eyes were drawn to his darkly tanned hands on the steering wheel, remembering how he had explored every inch of her body when he had made love to her.

He turned his head towards her. 'You look beautiful. The dress is a perfect fit and the colour suits you.'

Kristen tore her gaze from the glint of sexual awareness in his. She had chosen to wear a sky-blue silk jersey wrap dress to lunch with Sergio's father. Teamed with nude-coloured stiletto heels and matching bag, the outfit was elegant and yet the feel of the silk against her skin was incredibly sensual. 'It was kind of you to order the clothes,' she said stiltedly. 'When I go back to London I will, of course, reimburse you for them.' It would be another debt to add to the bureau where she kept her mother's outstanding bills, she thought ruefully.

Sergio put the car into gear and drove away from the villa. 'You don't owe me anything. It was my fault that you left London in a rush and didn't have time to pack your own clothes.'

It was the first reference he had made to the way he had taken Nico while Kristen had been asleep, and she thought she heard a faint apology in his voice.

'Will anyone else be at lunch besides your father?'

'Salvatore will be there with his daughter.'

'Rosa was only a few months old when I last saw her.' Kristen recalled his brother's pretty baby girl and beautiful wife, Adriana. 'What about Rosa's mother? Is Adriana away? I know she often went to Rome for modelling assignments.'

Sergio shot her a glance. 'Adriana is dead. She was killed in a car accident when Rosa was a year old.'

'Oh…how terrible! No wonder Salvatore looks so haggard.' What a cruel twist of fate that both the brothers' wives had died tragically young, Kristen mused. 'I noticed that he walks with a limp. Was he in the car when the accident happened?'

'Salvatore was driving them home from a dinner party. No one knows why he lost control of the car but it plunged over the edge of the mountain road they were travelling on. Adriana died instantly and Salvatore was seriously injured. My brother has no memory of the accident.' Sergio hesitated. 'He is wracked with guilt that it was his fault Adriana died, but I can't help wondering if his amnesia is an emotional response to the accident and the events leading up to it.'

'What do you mean?' Kristen asked curiously.

Sergio shrugged. 'I suspect that Salvatore's marriage was not as happy as everyone believed. He did not confide in me, but I sensed tension between him and Adriana, mainly over her decision to return to modelling and the fact that she left Rosa behind when she went to Rome for work. Perhaps they argued in the car that night and Salvatore was distracted. He is usually a careful driver. But he can't remember what happened and he blames himself that because of him his daughter is growing up without her mother.

'To make matters worse, it was confirmed when Rosa was eighteen months old that she is profoundly deaf.' Sergio sighed. 'I know Salvatore loves his little girl, but he seems unable to connect with Rosa, and I fear that she is becoming more and more introverted.'

He glanced over his shoulder to Nico, who was loudly singing one of his nursery songs. 'It will be good for Rosa to play with Nico. Salvatore rarely leaves his castle, and Rosa has few chances to meet other children.'

When they arrived at La Casa Bianca, a butler escorted them to the dining room where Tito was waiting. Kristen was shocked when she met Sergio's father, although she managed to hide her reaction. Four years ago Tito Castellano had been a formidable man, but a series of strokes had left him looking older and frail. His black eyes were still sharply assessing, though, and Kristen let out her pent-up breath when he finally turned his gaze from her to his son.

'Sergio, I cannot deny I was shocked when Salvatore told me I have a grandson. I understand that the boy is three years old, so why did I not learn about him until today?'

'It is a private matter between me and Kristen,' Sergio explained in a cool voice.

The slight frostiness between the two men that Kristen had noticed four years ago was still there, she realised. There was no expression in Sergio's eyes, but she was so attuned to him that she could sense his tension. Perhaps the fact that he had spent most of his childhood in America with his mother had made it hard for him to bond with his father. The thought made her wonder if the reason Sergio was determined to keep Nico in Sicily was so that he would have a closer relationship with his son than he had with Tito.

Tito's frown cleared as Nico stepped out from behind Kristen. 'So this is the boy. There is no doubt he is your son, Sergio—he is the image of you.' The old man's eyes gleamed. 'I had almost given up hope that you would do your duty to the family and the company—but finally you have pleased me by providing the next Castellano heir.' His gaze darted to Kristen. 'Now, all that is to be done is to organise the wedding.'

Struggling to hide her shock, Kristen waited for Sergio to tell his father that they had absolutely no plans to marry, but to her confusion he made no response to Tito's statement and instead held out a chair for her to sit down at the dining table.

Anger flared inside her. Well, if he wouldn't say something, she would! Sergio had lifted Nico onto a chair that had been fitted with an additional cushion so that the little boy could reach the table. Now, as Sergio sat down next to Kristen, she glared at him.

'I think you should make it clear that we…' she began, but the rest of her words were lost as Sergio's head swooped towards her and he dropped a hard kiss on her lips that stole her breath.

'I agree we should reassure my father that although there were problems in our relationship which led to you and Nico living in England, we are now both committed to putting our son's interests first and doing what is best for him. Isn't that so, *cara*?'

'Yes…but…' She broke off as, out of the corner of her eye, she saw Nico reach for the water jug. 'Wait, Nico, let me help you…' She spoke too late and watched resignedly as he knocked the jug over and water quickly soaked through the tablecloth.

'It doesn't matter. Let him come and sit here next to me.' Tito was clearly captivated by his grandson. 'Do you know who I am?' he asked the little boy. 'I am your *nonno*.'

'Nonno,' Nico repeated, and grinned at his grandfather.

Tito looked over at the pretty dark-haired little girl sitting beside Salvatore. 'It is good to hear a child talk. You should do more to help Rosa, Salvatore. She may be unable to hear, but she should learn to speak.'

'I am looking for a speech therapist to work on her language skills,' Salvatore replied curtly. His dark eyes showed no expression when he glanced at his daughter and Kristen felt a tug of compassion for the little girl who was growing up without her mother and clearly needed more support from her father.

For the rest of the lunch she concentrated on reminding Nico of his table manners, and when he had had enough to eat she took him to play in the garden and offered to take Rosa too. Nico seemed completely unconcerned that Rosa did not speak, and within a short time the two children had worked out a way of communicating with each other.

Kristen did not have an opportunity to talk to Sergio privately until they were in the car driving back to Casa Camelia. 'Why didn't you explain to your father that we are not in a relationship?' she demanded. 'He seems to have the crazy idea that we are going to get married. Why on earth didn't you deny it?'

Sergio parked outside the villa and immediately jumped out and went to help Nico out of the car. 'We'll discuss it later,' he said coolly. 'I'm going to take Nico swimming this afternoon.'

'That's not a good idea so soon after he was ill,' Kristen said immediately. 'I think he should take things easy for the rest of today.'

'I'd like to see you persuade him to slow down,' he murmured drily as they both watched Nico running up and down the driveway, pretending to be an aeroplane. Sergio gave her an intent look. 'You're going to have to get used to sharing him with me because I'm not going to walk out of his life, however much you might wish me to,' he added perceptively.

'Can you give me your word on that, Sergio? I'm scared you'll let him down.' Kristen admitted her greatest fear. 'Fatherhood is a big commitment, and you need to decide whether you want to be part of Nico's life for the long haul, or not at all.' She could not bear for Nico to grow close to Sergio and then be rejected by him, like she had been rejected by her stepfather.

He had hurt Kristen badly four years ago, Sergio recognised. He had not found it easy to share his feelings, let alone examine what those feelings were. But the situation was different now. They had a child together and, for Nico's sake, Sergio realised that he had to face the demons in his past so that he could build a future with his son and perhaps with Kristen too.

'You don't need to doubt my commitment to him,' he said quietly. 'I will be a devoted father to Nico.' He hesitated. 'I promise I will do nothing to make you regret that we met again, Kristen.'

Sergio's serious tone touched a chord inside Kristen and she blinked to dispel the tears that filled her eyes. 'I hope you're right,' she said gruffly. But as she followed him into the villa she wondered how they were going to resolve the issue of sharing custody of Nico when they lived in different countries—and different worlds—she thought with a rueful glance around the luxurious villa. Sergio had said that Casa Camelia was Nico's home, but it wasn't hers. She would only ever be a visitor here, her presence tolerated by Sergio because she was the mother of his son. The prospect seemed unbearable and she avoided his gaze, desperate to hide the fact that she was falling apart.

'Are you going to come swimming with us?' Sergio asked Kristen as he swung Nico into his arms and the little boy laughed delightedly. 'I'll take him to get changed and meet you by the pool in five minutes.'

'Actually, I won't come. I've got a headache and sitting out in the sun probably won't help it.' The excuse was not completely untrue. Kristen had a slight headache, but what hurt more was Nico's utter fascination with Sergio and the fact that he didn't seem to need her any more.

Sergio gave her a searching look. 'Well, if you change your mind you know where to find us. I'm sure Nico will want you to watch his first swimming lesson. I appreciate that you are finding it hard to share him with me,' he said heavily. 'But you have memories of him from the moment he was born, while I was deprived of being part of his life and I have to build my relationship with him starting from now. I don't want us to fight over him. For his sake we must find a way to put the past behind us and move forward.'

He was right, of course, and his words left Kristen feeling ashamed. She reminded herself that she had only kept Nico a secret because she had believed that Sergio was married, but the real truth was she had been devastated that he had not chased after her when she had left him four years ago.

Had she kept his son from him to hurt him as he had hurt her? The thought made her feel uncomfortable but she forced herself to be honest. Had she denied him his child because he hadn't loved her? He had every right to be angry, she acknowledged. But in fact Sergio had shown remarkable restraint and, rather than playing the blame game, he was more concerned with working out how they could both be parents to Nico.

She could not blame Sergio if he thought she was be-having like a spoilt child, Kristen decided fifteen min-utes later as she walked across the patio on her way to the pool. Nico's high-pitched voice and Sergio's deeper tones drifted over the screen of tall shrubs that gave the pool area privacy from the rest of the garden. The sweet scent of jasmine and honeysuckle hung thick in the air and the sun warmed Kristen's skin so that the prospect of a swim was inviting.

'Mummy…' Nico was sitting on the steps at the shal-low end of the pool and when he saw Kristen he jumped up and hurtled towards her, a wide smile on his face. 'I want you to come swimming with me and Papà, Mummy.'

Kristen caught his wriggling, damp body close and laughed a little unsteadily as she felt a familiar ache of love for her little boy. 'Okay, I will. Have you been having fun with Papà?' When Nico nodded fervently, she smiled and looked over at Sergio. 'Good,' she said softly, 'I'm glad.'

His answering smile lifted her heart. She felt her pulse race at the sight of him wearing a pair of black swim shorts. Droplets of water glistened on his broad, tanned shoulders and as she watched he ducked beneath the sur-face of the pool and came up again, pushing his wet hair back from his brow.

'Is the water cold?'

'Not cold enough, unfortunately,' he drawled. His dark eyes glinted. 'Not when you look so gorgeous and incredibly tempting in that bikini.'

Kristen blushed and glanced down at the bikini which she had found with the other clothes he had bought for her. It consisted of two tiny pieces of jade-green Lycra and was far more daring than anything she would have chosen.

'You chose it,' she reminded him.

'And now I'm going to have to swim at least forty lengths to try and get rid of my frustration,' he said ruefully. 'Why don't you stay with Nico and let him show you how well he can swim with armbands?'

It was all about compromise, Kristen mused as she played in the shallow end with Nico while Sergio thrashed up and down the pool. She appreciated that he had given her time to be alone with Nico to prove that he didn't want to monopolize the little boy's attention. For the first time since she had arrived in Sicily, determined to snatch back her son, a sense of calm settled over her and she was even able to fool herself that everything would be all right.

The fragile feeling of hope lasted for the rest of the afternoon. Nico clearly loved having the attention of both his parents and Kristen discovered that sharing responsibility with another adult gave her a chance to relax and enjoy herself. Eventually Sergio carried their tired son back to the house and, after he'd had his tea and a bath, Nico was ready for bed.

Luisa, Rosa's nanny, arrived just as Kristen had finished reading him a story. 'Salvatore offered to put Rosa to bed tonight, and suggested that I should come and see if you need any help with Nico,' she explained, speaking

in fluent English. 'It is good that he is feeling better today
and was able to meet his grandfather.'

'Yes, Tito seemed much taken with him,' Kristen said,
remembering how Sergio's father had not taken his eyes
off Nico during lunch.

'Of course! Signor Castellano is delighted. For many
years he has hoped that Sergio would provide an heir who
will one day inherit the company with Salvatore's daughter.' Luisa shrugged. 'My cousin works as Tito's cook, and
she heard rumours among the household staff that Tito had
delayed giving Sergio the permanent role of joint CEO of
the Castellano Group with his twin brother, and chose instead to name only Salvatore as his successor. But that is
to change now that Sergio has a son. Tito has instructed
the company's lawyers to upgrade Sergio's status to CEO,
the same as Salvatore, and I understand that Tito is impatient for the two of you to marry so that Nico becomes
a legitimate heir.'

Luisa smiled, unaware that Kristen's lack of response
was because she was too shocked to speak. Her mind was
reeling, but everything Luisa had told her made horrible
sense. 'I was going to offer to sit with Nico,' the nanny
said, 'but he has already fallen asleep.'

'It's not necessary for you to stay, thank you.' Somehow
Kristen managed to keep a lid on her anger until the nanny
had gone, but as she marched next door into Sergio's room
her temper reached boiling point.

'Did Nico settle okay?' He strolled over to meet her,
looking unfairly sexy in tailored black trousers and a white
silk shirt that contrasted with his bronzed complexion.
With his silky hair falling forward onto his brow and his
mouth curved into a sensual smile, he looked every inch a
billionaire playboy, and jealousy stabbed Kristen through

her heart as she wondered how many women must have shared his bed.

'I thought we would have dinner on the terrace…like we used to do,' he said softly. 'But I'm feeling a little over-dressed.'

His eyes glinted with amusement and something else that made Kristen catch her breath as his gaze roamed over her bikini-clad body. Despite the fact that she had slipped on a chiffon shirt which matched the bikini, she felt at a disadvantage when he was fully dressed, especially when a quick glance downwards revealed that her nipples were clearly visible, jutting beneath the clingy Lycra bra top.

She pulled the edges of the gauzy shirt together in an attempt to hide her treacherous body from him. 'Why have you not told your father the truth about us? He is still under the illusion that we intend to marry. But I suppose it suits you not to clarify the misunderstanding,' she ploughed on without giving him the opportunity to speak, 'just as it suited you to bring Nico here. I understand now why you were so determined to bring him to Sicily.'

'Do you?' Sergio's face was enigmatic but his voice was cool as he drawled, 'Why don't you enlighten me?'

'Luisa told me that your father refused to name you as his successor jointly with Salvatore until you produced an heir. How convenient for you that you discovered your son, especially when Tito's health is failing. Luisa said she has heard that Tito is now preparing to upgrade you to CEO of the Castellano Group, the same as your brother.' She gave a bitter laugh. 'And to think you convinced me that you wanted to be a proper father to Nico. I should have remembered that you usually avoid commitment like the plague. Thank goodness he hasn't had time to form a close bond with you. I'm going to take him back to England before you have a chance to hurt him.'

She swung away from Sergio but, before she could take a step, he gripped her shoulder and spun her back round to face him. 'What nonsense is this?' he grated. 'I would never harm a hair on Nico's head.'

'No, but you could break his heart. He has really taken to you and doesn't stop talking about his daddy. He won't understand that he comes second in your life, and that the company is the only thing you care about. You brought Nico to Sicily because your father wouldn't name you as his successor until you produced an heir.'

'And you know this because Luisa told you? You believe the word of a member of staff who does not even work at my father's house, and who is well known for her habit of spreading gossip, which in this case is completely unfounded.'

Sergio had not raised his voice, but somehow his quiet tone was infinitely more dangerous. His jaw was rigid with tension and Kristen realised he was furious.

She bit her lip as it belatedly occurred to her that she might have been too ready to jump to conclusions. 'Do you deny it?'

'Of course I damn well deny it. My father stipulated years ago that when he dies, or when bad health prevents him from carrying out his role as head of the company, Salvatore and I will take over from him and we will have equal responsibility. It is true that Tito made some minor alterations to his will recently, and perhaps that is where the rumours have arisen from. But it is *not* true that my position within the company is dependent on me having an heir.'

His dark eyes glimmered with anger as he stared at Kristen's startled face. 'I brought Nico to Sicily because I want the chance to get to know my son. I know what it's like to grow up without a father. It might suit you to deny it, but Nico will benefit from having a male role model. He needs his father, and I…' he swallowed convulsively '…I love him already,' he said roughly. 'I will *never* let him down the way you seem to think I will.'

Shaken by the fervency of Sergio's words, Kristen found that she believed him and felt guilty for accusing him without first checking the facts. 'I'm sorry,' she said huskily. 'I just wanted to protect Nico. I was stunned when your father mentioned a wedding. But I suppose it's understandable that he assumes we are going to get married.'

'He didn't make an assumption. I told him that I intend to marry you.'

Shock caused her heart to jolt painfully against her ribs. 'What…*why*? Why on earth did you do that?'

Sergio's brows lifted in an arrogant expression that made Kristen itch to slap him.

'Do you have a better idea for how we can both be parents to our son and spare him the uncertainty of a custody battle?'

'I can think of a dozen ideas that do not involve marriage between two people who don't…'

'Don't what, *mia bella*?' Sergio tightened his grip on her shoulder and pulled her towards him, crushing her slender frame against his hard body. 'Don't desire one another? Don't hunger for one another night and day? Because if that were the case, I agree the marriage would be doomed to failure. But I dare you to deny the passion that ignites between us with one look, one touch…one kiss.'

His dark head swooped and he captured her mouth, forcing her lips apart with the bold thrust of his tongue and kissing her with fiery passion that lit a flame inside Kristen. Her body responded to its master, but some tiny part of her sanity still lingered, and when he pushed her shirt over her shoulders she tore her mouth from his.

'What you are talking about is just sex. It's not the basis of a marriage…Sergio…put me down!' She beat her hands on his chest as he lifted her as easily as though she were a rag doll and dropped her onto the bed.

'It's a start,' he said, and the quiet intensity of his voice sent a tremor through her. 'Desire seems a very good reason why I should make you my wife.'

CHAPTER TEN

SERGIO'S PROPOSAL WAS four years too late, Kristen thought bitterly. Not that he had actually proposed. He had told his father he intended to marry her, and as a secondary thought he had casually let her know what he planned. Her anger brimmed over. Four years ago she would have leapt at the chance to be his wife, but his arrogant assumption that she was still the silly, love-struck girl she had been then fuelled her resentment and hurt. Because the real reason, the only reason, he had decided to marry her was for Nico's sake. And, much as Kristen adored her son, she would not endure a loveless marriage that would be all the worse because in her heart she acknowledged that she had never stopped loving Sergio.

What kind of a fool did that make her? She hated herself for loving him. Hated the way her body was so utterly enslaved by him that one kiss was all it took to make her melt in his arms. She realised with a flash of insight that he was always in control because she allowed him to be. Four years ago she had been too young and awed by him to make her own demands and fight for what she wanted in their relationship. But no more. She was a strong and independent woman now; she'd had to be as a single mother trying to hold down a career and bring up a child. She had no intention of marrying Sergio simply because he would find it convenient. But at the same time she could not deny her desire for him. Her breasts felt heavy and she could feel the warm flood of her arousal between her legs. She wanted to make love with him, but on her terms, not his.

He knelt over her, his dark eyes raging with a primitive hunger to possess his woman.

'I desired you from the first time I watched you dancing on the sand. You felt the attraction between us that day too, and it has never faded. You want me as much as I want you,' he said harshly, and with one swift movement he unfastened her bikini top and tugged it away from her breasts.

Kristen's anger exploded. She pushed against his chest, taking him by surprise so that he was momentarily unbalanced, giving her the chance to roll away from him. With the grace and surprising strength gained from years of gymnastics training, she pushed him onto his back and straddled his hips.

'I'm sick of being manipulated by you,' she said fiercely. 'You always want everything to be your way. You snatched Nico and forced me to leave my job and life in London and come to Sicily. But you won't force me to marry you.'

She shook her tumbling mane of blonde hair over her shoulders and sat back a little so that her breasts thrust provocatively forward. Sergio inhaled sharply and the sensation of his arousal stirring beneath her made her feel triumphant that she had power over him. 'You fall far short of what I want from a husband,' she told him. 'But as a lover you are first class.'

Sergio's eyes narrowed. 'Is that so? Are you saying you want to have sex with me but nothing else?'

'How does it feel, Sergio?' she taunted. 'Does it make you feel good to know that the only part of you I'm interested in is your body? That's how you made me feel during our affair.' Her voice shook betrayingly. 'I was good enough for sex but not for you to share your feelings with.'

To her surprise, he did not refute her accusation but sighed deeply. 'I'm sorry I made you feel like that and I'm sorry I hurt you.'

He could not change the past, Sergio thought heavily. He had not met Kristen's emotional needs and he could understand why she was afraid that he would fail Nico in the same way that he had failed her. Somehow he had to show her that *he* could change. He would not find it easy to open up when he had kept his emotions locked away for most of his life, but everything was at stake here and he was willing to try.

He looked into her bright blue eyes and felt an inexplicable ache in his chest. She was so beautiful. His gaze dropped to her small, firm breasts with their puckered nipples and a white-hot shaft of desire ripped through him but, instead of taking control and flipping her onto her back, he relaxed against the pillows and spread his arms wide like an indolent sultan waiting to be pleasured by his favourite concubine.

'If sex is what you want, then take me, Krissie. I'm all yours.'

Sergio's soft words stabbed Kristen through the heart. He had never been hers, not in the way she longed for. His heart and soul belonged solely to himself, and perhaps, she thought with a pang, to his dead wife. Passion was all he had ever given her. So why not accept what he offered and take her pleasure with his virile body, if that was all she could have of him?

The hard glitter in his eyes betrayed his hunger, but amazingly he seemed prepared to allow her to take the lead. A heady sense of power swept through her and a desire to tease and torment him as he had done so often to her. She held his gaze as she unfastened his shirt buttons and pushed the material aside to expose his darkly tanned chest, and leaned forward so that the tips of her breasts brushed across his wiry chest hairs.

The sensation made her nipples tingle and harden. The contrast between her milky-pale breasts and his bronzed skin was incredibly erotic. Colour flared on his cheekbones and his breath hissed between his teeth as her hair fell forward and brushed lightly over his naked torso.

'Witch,' he said raggedly as she moved lower so that her soft hair and her pebble-hard nipples stroked a path over his abdomen. With nimble fingers she deftly undid the zip of his trousers and when her hands slid beneath his boxers and closed around his throbbing arousal Sergio gave a low groan. He knew he was close to the edge and almost gave in to the temptation to roll over and drag her beneath him so that he could find the relief he craved, but he managed to hold back. It was true that when they had made love previously it had always been on his terms, and he had never given himself completely. But if he was ever going to win Kristen's trust he must prove that he did not want to dominate her.

The flick of her tongue over the sensitive tip of his manhood made him clench his muscles to stop himself from falling apart. His body shook as he fought the waves of pleasure that rolled over him when she took his swollen shaft into the moist cavern of her mouth.

'What does it feel like to know that this is all that exists between us?' she murmured.

If it was true, it would hurt him maybe more deeply than any pain he had known in his life, Sergio acknowledged. But he had heard the tremor in her voice and recognised the inherent tenderness of her caresses, and he was certain that she felt more for him than simply sexual desire. It was in her kiss when she arched above him and claimed his mouth with heart-shaking passion. He glimpsed it briefly in her eyes when she guided herself down onto him and took his rigid length inside her, inch by inch, pausing while her internal muscles stretched to accommodate him. Her lashes lowered and hid her expression. But he thought he had seen love there. He wasn't sure. But it gave him hope that perhaps there was a chance he could win her back.

Desire took over wild and wanton as she rode him, her slender body moving with instinctive grace while he cupped her breasts and played with her nipples, increasing her pleasure, escalating her excitement so that she threw her head back and made love to him with an abandonment that touched his soul. They climaxed simultaneously, breathing hard and fast in those moments of sheer physical ecstasy, their hearts thundering in unison when she collapsed on top of him and Sergio wrapped his arms around her and threaded his fingers in her hair.

Eventually the world righted itself and Kristen lifted herself off Sergio and moved away from him. It was ridiculous to feel shy, but she couldn't bring herself to meet his gaze. Making love with him had been heaven, but now the gates of hell beckoned as she wondered if she had given herself away. Had he guessed that desire was only one part of what she felt for him? She had taunted him that sex was all she wanted from him, but she had a horrible feeling that he knew she had been lying.

He confirmed her fears when he propped himself on one elbow and gave her a lazy smile. 'I think it's fair to say we have proved irrefutably that desire is an excellent reason for us to get married.' He paused for a heartbeat before adding softly, 'Another reason is that we forgot to use protection, so unless you are on the Pill there's a chance you could have conceived my child.' He met her stunned gaze with an enigmatic expression. 'I'll start to organise the wedding immediately.'

Dear God! How could she have been so stupid? Feeling numb, Kristen slid off the bed and wrapped Sergio's shirt around her. Without saying a word, she walked into the adjoining sitting room and stood by the window, which looked out over the lake. The setting sun had turned the water to gold and beyond the lake the Sicilian countryside was bathed in mellow light while in the distance tall pine trees were silhouetted against the pink sky. The beauty of the scene, the feeling of being insignificant in the vastness of the universe, intensified the ache in Kristen's heart.

She heard Sergio come up behind her and when he placed a hand on her shoulder she spun round to face him. 'How can we get married when a day ago you believed I was responsible for the bruises on Nico's legs?' she said shakily. 'We are virtually strangers. If you knew me at all you would have realised that I would cut my heart out rather than hurt him.' She swallowed. 'Do you have any idea how I felt when I realised you had taken him? What kind of relationship would we have when there is no trust between us?'

The shadows in her eyes warned Sergio that she deserved to hear the truth, even though that meant finally opening himself up and revealing the grim secrets of his childhood.

'I trust you,' he said intently. 'But I admit that when I saw the bruises on Nico my reactions were purely instinctive. My only thought was to rescue him.'

'You believed he needed to be rescued from me?' Kristen blinked back the hot tears burning her eyes. 'Do you really think I am such a terrible mother?'

'No. Not now that I have watched you with him and seen how deeply you care for him. But in London...'

Sergio hesitated and took a swift breath '…I wondered if you were like my mother.'

'I…I don't understand.' Looking into Sergio's dark eyes, Kristen had the strange feeling that she was hovering on the edge of a precipice and for some reason her heart was thumping.

'My mother used to beat me when I was a child.'

The words circled around Kristen but she could not grasp them or make sense of them. Sergio seemed to re-alise that she was too shocked to respond and continued in a flat voice, 'The bruises on Nico's legs reminded me of the marks my mother used to leave when she caned me. When I was just a few years older than Nico I used to hope that my father would come and take me home to Sicily. I was desperate for his protection…but he never came.' His throat worked as he fought to retain his iron self-control.

'I guess I went a little mad. I had just discovered my son, and the possibility that he might be physically and emotionally at risk brought back memories of my child-hood that, unfortunately, I can never forget. I wasn't think-ing straight,' he admitted. 'I have spent my life wondering if my father did not love me and that was why he failed to protect me. I was determined to protect Nico so that he would never have reason to doubt my love for him.'

It was strange to hear Sergio talk of love. Kristen had often wondered why he apparently lacked the normal range of emotions that most people had, and she had longed to break through his air of detachment and discover if he re-ally was the empty shell he gave the impression of being. Now she knew. And the truth was utterly heartbreaking. The lines of strain on his face revealed a man who was struggling to control his emotions—and who could blame him? she thought sadly.

'Why did your mother…?' She could not go on, feeling physically sick as she imagined Sergio as a young boy, being beaten by the person who should have cared for him the most. It made her want to run to Nico's bedroom and hug him tight. She would give her life to protect her little boy and she was able to sympathise with how Sergio must have felt when he had seen bruises on Nico's legs. It was understandable that after his experiences as a child he had wanted to protect his son, but it still hurt that he had believed Nico had needed protection from her.

'I don't know why she did it,' Sergio said heavily. 'I think she was frustrated by her lack of success as an actress, and she had an issue with alcohol. She could be very loving, but I always felt I was walking on a knife-edge and the slightest thing could send her into a violent rage. She told me once that her father used to beat her and her mother after he had been drinking. While she was married to my father she seemed to be a caring mother to me and my brother. But when she took me to America she started to drink heavily. I used to think she beat me because she hated me. She seemed to enjoy making me cry, and so I learned to keep my emotions bottled up. It became a matter of pride not to show my feelings…and as I grew older the habit of hiding what I felt became second nature.'

Kristen felt a lump in her throat. It was no wonder that, after years of suffering physical abuse, Sergio had erected defences as a means of self-protection from being hurt emotionally.

'Why didn't your father help you? Surely, if you had told him what was happening, he would have tried to get you back?'

'I had no contact with him from the age of five. My mother told me that it was my father's choice. Years later, when I returned to Sicily, Tito insisted that he had tried to keep in touch and my mother had prevented him.'

Sergio's jaw clenched. 'Frankly, I suspect that he didn't try very hard.'

'So why did your mother allow you to go back to your father when you were a teenager?'

He hesitated, and Kristen sensed that he was struggling to talk about his past. 'I beat up her boyfriend.' Sergio grimaced when he heard Kristen gasp. 'The guy hit me, and I snapped and hit him back, breaking his nose in the process. For a few seconds I was overcome by sheer rage and I wanted to kill the guy...' he swallowed convulsively '...and my mother too. But afterwards I was ashamed that I had allowed my emotions to get the better of me. I must have scared my mother because she decided she couldn't cope with my anger issues and sent me back to Sicily. But it was too late to build a relationship with Tito, and even with my twin brother. We had been apart for ten years, and I was jealous of Salvatore's closeness to our father. In my mind, Salvatore was the favoured son. I felt I had to prove myself to Tito, especially in business, and show him that I deserved to be his successor just as much as my brother.'

'So you worked obsessively,' Kristen said, gaining sudden insight into why the Castellano Group had been more important to him than anything else, including his relationship with her. Did he still feel the need to prove his worth to his father? she wondered. If so, where would Nico come in his priorities?

He must have read her thoughts because he said quickly, 'Nothing is more important to me than building a relationship with my son. Fortunately, he is young enough that he will hopefully not remember that I wasn't around for his baby years. It is not too late for me and Nico—as it was with me and my father. I will work hard to make up for the time I lost with him.'

The accusation that the lost years were her fault hung

between them and Kristen felt even guiltier now that Sergio had told her about his childhood. 'I did what I thought was best,' she said stiffly. 'You were so distant at the hospital after I'd had the miscarriage, and I truly believed you did not want a child with me.'

'The fault was mine, not yours,' he assured her. 'I was so well-practised at hiding my emotions and it didn't occur to me that you needed to see that I was grieving for our baby too.'

Kristen bit her lip as a dozen 'if onlys' ran through her mind. If only Sergio had confided in her during their affair then she might have understood why he seemed so coldly unemotional. If only she had remained in Sicily with him, instead of going back to England in high dudgeon because he had only asked her to be his mistress, then she would have told him she was still pregnant with her dead baby's twin, and maybe he would have married her rather than the beautiful Sicilian woman whose photo he kept in his bedroom.

She turned away to the window and saw that the sun had sunk below the horizon while they had been talking and a few faint stars were appearing in the purple sky. Somehow the beauty of the heavens seemed tainted by the ugliness of Sergio's revelations and she felt an aching sadness for him, for her and for the course of events that had led them to be on opposite sides, each fighting to be full-time parents to their son.

'When you came to live with your father, did you tell him how your mother had treated you?'

'No.' He shrugged. 'I have explained that we are not close…and there was a part of me that wondered if Patti's mistreatment of me was somehow my fault. It was not something I wanted to talk about with Tito. And I couldn't say anything to Salvatore. He was already angry that our mother had abandoned him when he was a young child. In many ways Salvatore's childhood was as unhappy as mine. He told me that our father was very bitter after Patti left. Tito focused all his time and energy on the company and shut off his emotions. It must be a family trait,' Sergio said grimly. 'I couldn't tell Salvatore that the mother he had missed so desperately when he was a child was a spiteful, unpleasant woman.

'Patti died a year after I returned to Sicily—she drowned in the bath after a heavy drinking session. My brother and I didn't have the chance to ask her why she had treated us the way she did. I was an angry and confused young man, but thankfully one person understood me. I confided in Annamaria and she helped me come to terms with my past.'

Kristen had never heard Sergio speak in such a gentle tone, and she felt a stab of jealousy. 'Who is Annamaria?' The photograph of the dark-haired woman in Sergio's bedroom leapt into her mind, and she knew the answer to her question before he could answer. 'She was your wife, wasn't she?'

'Yes.' Sergio hesitated. 'I think I should explain about Annamaria.'

'There's no need.' Kristen stalled him quickly. The green-eyed demon inside her couldn't bear to hear details of the woman he had married soon after their own relationship had ended. She swung around to the window and crossed her arms in front of her, subconsciously retreating from him as he had done to her in the past.

He must have loved Annamaria to have told her about his childhood. In stark contrast, he had never spoken about personal matters to *her* during their affair, she thought bleakly. Admittedly, he had confided in her now, but only because he needed to explain why he had snatched Nico. He had also asked her to marry him, but not because he loved her. He wanted security for Nico, and she couldn't blame him for that after hearing about his desperately sad childhood.

But sexual compatibility was not a firm basis for marriage. What would happen if Sergio's desire for her faded? She couldn't bear the prospect of being his wife in name only while he had affairs with other women. Oh, she was sure he would be discreet, but she would be so unhappy, like her mother had been with her stepfather.

'I know I hurt you four years ago,' he said quietly. 'I did not realise how much until you told me that you believed I did not want the baby you miscarried.'

He placed his hands on her shoulders and turned her towards him, his jaw tightening when he felt how stiffly she was holding herself. She had put up barriers between them and he could hardly blame her when he had done the same during their affair, Sergio acknowledged heavily. But although she was wary of him she adored Nico and surely she must see that for his sake they had to put the past behind them.

'I promise I can change from the person you knew four years ago,' he said intently. 'I have changed already. I no longer feel the need to prove myself to my father. Being Nico's father is more important to me than any business deal.'

The rigidity of her shoulders told him she was not reassured, and there was a wary expression in her bright blue eyes that warned him he must curb his impatience. He had sprung the idea of marriage on her and, although to him it was the obvious solution that would allow Nico to live with both his parents, Kristen clearly had reservations. He could hardly blame her after he had revealed the abuse he had suffered as a child, he acknowledged bleakly.

'There is evidence which seems to show that in some

cases a person who was badly treated during childhood can go on to mistreat their own children,' he said quietly. 'But I swear I would never harm Nico in any way. If I believed there was even the slightest chance that I could lose my temper with him I would give up my right to be his father.'

Kristen was unbearably moved by the pain she heard in his voice. 'You have already shown yourself to be a brilliant dad and I trust absolutely that you will always take care of him.'

'Then why are you hesitating about accepting my proposal? The quicker we get married the quicker Nico will settle into his new life here at Casa Camelia.'

Sergio's statement set off alarm bells in Kristen. 'That's a very big assumption you have made. Why would we have to live in Sicily? I have a life in London, a career that I enjoy and a wide circle of friends, many of whom have children who are Nico's playmates.'

He shrugged. 'He would make friends here.'

'Probably, but that's not the point.' Frustration surged through Kristen. 'You told me you've changed from the man you were four years ago, but I can't see much evidence of that. You still want everything to be your way. If we were to marry, why couldn't we live in England?'

'I need to live here because the Castellano Group is based in Sicily.'

As soon as the words left his mouth Sergio knew he had made a mistake. The flash of anger in Kristen's eyes warned him he was in danger of losing any headway he had made with her.

'So, just as it did four years ago, the company comes first in your list of priorities, and if I agreed to marry you I would have to change my whole life to fit in with yours.'

Her scathing tone riled him. 'You make it sound as though Casa Camelia is a hovel, and moving here would be a terrible hardship. But it's a hell of a lot better than the rabbit hutch you call home in London. As for your job— you would not need to work and you could spend more time with Nico. Perhaps you could even take up gymnastics again.'

Sergio had played his trump card, Kristen acknowledged. Much as she enjoyed her job, she would love to be a full-time mum to Nico, at least until he started school. And she had often thought she would like to become a gymnastics coach, but she had never had time to attend the training courses while she worked full-time.

But marriage was such a massive step.

'I'm not convinced that a marriage of convenience would be right for us or for Nico. What if we were to divorce in a few years' time? That would be more painful for him than if we organise how we can both be a part of his life while leading separate lives of our own.'

The conversation was not heading in the direction Sergio wanted. It struck him forcibly that he hated the idea of Kristen living a separate life from him in London. She was so beautiful that she would undoubtedly attract a lot of male attention, and there would be nothing to stop her having lovers, maybe even marrying some other guy. Jealousy burned like acid in his gut. He was tempted to seize her in his arms and kiss her until she was mindless with desire, prove that the blazing passion they shared was special—just as she was special to him. But the determined tilt of her chin reminded him that she was not a pushover, and so he dropped his hands from her shoulders and looked deeply into her eyes.

'Nico's well-being is not the only reason I want to marry you, Krissie. And I am not contemplating us getting divorced. I'm talking about making a long-term commitment to you and to the future that I very much hope we will share. I would also like us to have more children. It would be good for Nico to grow up with siblings.'

Her sharp intake of breath warned him that he was going too fast. 'But I understand your concerns,' he said quickly, 'and I think we should put the idea of marriage on hold for a while and spend time getting to know each other again.'

Sergio smiled suddenly, breaking the tension and causing Kristen's heart to perform a somersault as he worked his sensual magic on her. 'What do you say, *cara*? Will you give me a chance?'

What could she say? she thought ruefully. She was still reeling from his statement that Nico was not the only reason he had suggested they get married. What on earth had he meant? With a helpless shrug she said huskily, 'I guess so. Yes.'

CHAPTER ELEVEN

SPENDING A DAY on Sergio's luxury yacht, which boasted a swimming pool, a Jacuzzi and cinema on its list of amenities, promised to be a relaxing experience. Spending a day on Sergio's yacht accompanied by an inquisitive, daredevil three-year-old boy was rather less relaxing, but it had still been a wonderful day, Kristen mused as the *Dolphin* dropped anchor in a small bay close to a private beach belonging to the Castellano estate.

'This is as close to the shore as we can go,' Sergio said as he strode across the deck. Wearing cut-off denim shorts and a fine cotton shirt left open to reveal his darkly tanned torso, he was one gorgeous sexy male and Kristen felt a delicious coiling sensation in the pit of her stomach at the thought that tonight he would make love to her. He had been away on a business trip the previous week and after five nights of aching frustration she was impatient to feel him inside her. Just the thought of his hard arousal nudging between her thighs was enough to make her breasts grow heavy, and she was glad that the sarong she had wrapped around her hid her pebble-hard nipples.

'We'll have to take the motor launch across to the beach. I'll hang on to Nico because he's as wriggly as an eel.' Sergio grinned as he swung his son into his arms. 'I want you to promise me that you will sit still when we go in the little boat, *piccolo*.'

'I will, Papà,' Nico said earnestly.

'Good boy.'

Watching her son rest his head on his father's shoulder, Kristen acknowledged that the bond between them grew stronger with every day. Nico hero-worshipped his daddy, and Sergio's love for his little boy shone in his eyes and was evident in the tenderness of his voice. It was wonderful to hear Nico laughing again, she thought. He was no longer the sad little boy he had been in London, and his grief over his nana's death had been forgotten in the excitement of getting to know his father.

Nico obediently sat still on Sergio's lap as the motor launch skimmed towards the shore and only once did he lean over the edge to try to catch the spray, causing his parents a few moments panic.

'He's utterly fearless,' Sergio said with rueful pride in his voice when they reached the beach and he set Nico down on the sand. 'I think we'll have to postpone another trip on the *Dolphin* until my nerves have recovered.' He smiled at Kristen as they strolled along the beach after Nico, who had shot off in front. 'What did the two of you get up to while I was away?'

'I took him swimming in the pool every day. He's only been learning for a few weeks since we arrived here, but he's almost ready to try without his armbands.' She gave him a quick glance. 'He really missed you.'

'The business trip to Hong Kong was booked months ago and I couldn't get out of going,' he said quickly. 'But I won't go away again or, if I do, I'll take Nico and you with me. I missed both of you.'

Sergio caught hold of her hand and wrapped his fingers around hers as they continued to walk towards the beach hut. Kristen let out a soft sigh. The day had been perfect so far, but then every day that she spent with Sergio was wonderful. The easy companionship that had developed between them reminded her of the early days of their affair. When they had first met he had been recovering from a sports injury which had meant that he'd had to take time off work. They had quickly become lovers, and she remembered they had spent lazy days on the beach and nights of incredible passion back at Casa Camelia. His commitment to the Castellano Group had not been a problem at first, but once he'd returned to his role as head of the property development side of the company their time together had been limited to nights of wild sex, and Kristen had felt hurt that his only interest seemed to be in her body.

Would the same thing happen again if she agreed to marry him? The evidence so far was that he had changed from the man he had been four years ago, she acknowledged. He only went to his office for a few hours a day, and was always home by mid-afternoon to play with Nico. She had come to love the hours that the three of them spent together almost as much as the nights when Sergio made love to her so beautifully that sometimes she had to blink back her tears before he saw them.

She suddenly realised that he was talking to her, and quickly dragged her mind back to the present.

'Did Rosa come over to play with Nico?'

'Yes, Salvatore brought her so that she could swim. He says Rosa has come out of her shell a little since she has had Nico as a playmate.'

Sergio frowned. 'I'm surprised my brother brought her, rather than the nanny. Perhaps Salvatore enjoyed being with you while the children played.'

Something in his tone made Kristen stop walking, and she turned to face him. 'I like your brother, and it was nice to chat to him. He is frustrated that he is still suffering from amnesia and can't remember anything of the accident. He blames himself for Adriana's death.' She watched Sergio's frown deepen and shook her head. 'Surely you can't be jealous of my friendship with Salvatore?'

'I am jealous of any man who looks at you,' he growled. While she was digesting this statement he jerked her against him and tangled his fingers in her long hair. 'I guard my possessions fiercely, *cara*.'

He brought his mouth down on hers and kissed her with a savage hunger that triggered an instant reaction in Kristen. She had long ago given up trying to resist him, and wound her arms around his neck while she kissed him back with all the pent-up passion that had built to an intolerable level during the five nights that he had been away.

'*Dio!* If we were alone I would take you right here on the sand,' he muttered when he eventually lifted his head and dragged oxygen into his lungs. 'I wish we weren't hosting a dinner party tonight. Maybe we could cancel it?'

Kristen wasn't sure how she felt about Sergio regarding her as one of his possessions. There was something very primitive about the idea of being owned by him. But, for all his effort to be a 'new man', he was at heart a hot-blooded Sicilian male, she thought ruefully, and she could not deny a little thrill of pleasure when he wrapped his arms around her and crushed her against his chest so that she could feel the strong beat of his heart.

'Of course we can't cancel. I'm looking forward to meeting your friends, Benito and Lia, and I really liked Gerardo and Flavia when we had dinner with them last week.' Kristen gave an impish smile that made Sergio catch his breath. 'I promise the anticipation will be worthwhile,' she murmured, trailing her fingertips down his chest and abdomen and stopping at the waistband of his shorts.

'Witch,' he groaned, and kissed her again. From along the beach they heard Nico calling for his *papà*. 'I have to go,' Sergio said regretfully.

'Go away on another business trip, do you mean?'

'No. Go and build my son a sandcastle like I promised him.'

She laughed. 'You'd better hurry up then.'

As she watched father and son digging in the sand Kristen's thoughts returned to the phone call she had had that morning from Steph, her boss at the physiotherapy clinic in London. Steph had asked when she planned to return to work.

'I'm not sure yet. I'll let you know in a couple of days,' Kristen had replied. She appreciated that over the last few weeks Sergio had made a lot of effort to allay her concerns about marrying him. Steph's question had been lurking in the back of her mind all day, and the conclusion she had reached was frightening and yet glaringly obvious.

It was almost midnight before the dinner party guests departed. The evening had been fun, Kristen mused as she walked into the master bedroom that she had shared with Sergio for the past weeks. The two married couples they had dined with had young children, and Kristen had arranged play-dates so that Nico could make new friends. He had settled at Casa Camelia amazingly quickly and, although she seemed to spend her life chasing after him to cover him in sun-cream, his arms and legs were already nut-brown and he looked much more Sicilian than English.

Returning to their old life in London was not an option. It wouldn't be fair to uproot Nico and it wasn't what she wanted either, Kristen acknowledged. She walked over to the dressing table and stared at the reflection of the slender, elegant woman wearing a stunning designer gown of black taffeta that was a perfect foil for her blonde hair, which was caught up in a loose chignon on top of her head. The dress was strapless, floor-length and showed off her tiny waist, while the low-cut neckline revealed the pale upper slopes of her breasts.

Sergio had brought the dress back from his trip especially for her to wear tonight. With it he had given her a diamond necklace, and she had caught her breath when he had fastened the single strand of exquisite glittering stones around her neck. But her heart had raced faster still when he had stared into her eyes and told her how beautiful she looked. There had been something in his expression that she could not define, but it gave her hope that the decision she had made was the right one.

Perhaps it was natural that she felt nervous, she thought, as she wandered restlessly around the room. She wished he would hurry up and come to bed. Unlike four years ago, it was unusual for him to take a business call late at night, but an urgent problem had needed his attention.

Her gaze fell on the photograph of the dark-haired young woman on Sergio's desk. He had loved Annamaria and, recalling the soft tone of his voice when he had spoken about her, it seemed very likely that he still did. Biting her lip, Kristen did a reality check. Sergio had asked her to marry him for various reasons, number one being that he believed it would be best for Nico and number two because he desired her, but he had never mentioned love.

She sighed. After the way his mother had treated him as a child, it was understandable that he found it hard to show his feelings and perhaps it was unrealistic to hope that he would fall in love with her. She couldn't blame him for guarding his emotions. But she had sensed over the past few weeks that he did care for her, and maybe in time his feelings would develop into love.

Maybe, if she told him how she felt about him…? Kristen's heart lurched at the prospect of opening herself up to being rejected once again. Sergio had ripped her heart out four years ago, and she was still haunted by how her stepfather had let her down when she had needed his support.

She had two choices, Kristen realised. She could be a coward and carry on hiding her feelings for Sergio, or she could take charge of her own destiny and find the courage to tell him she loved him. Yes, she risked being hurt, but she had been hurt before and survived. Honesty was the best policy, but did she have the nerve to offer her heart to Sergio?

'You look very pensive. What are you thinking about?'

She turned her head at the sound of his voice and watched him close the bedroom door. He looked incredibly sexy in black tailored trousers and a black silk shirt, and she was reminded of when she had seen him at the Hotel Royale in London. It seemed so long ago, but it was only a matter of weeks since she had gatecrashed his party and he had crashed back into her life.

'I have something to tell you. I found out while you were away that there are no repercussions from our carelessness a couple of weeks ago. I'm not pregnant.'

'I see.' Sergio's tone gave nothing away and Kristen had no idea if he was as disappointed by the news as she was.

He strolled over to her and she saw a familiar glint in his gaze as his eyes roamed over the sexy black dress. 'Did I tell you how stunning you look tonight, *mia bella*?'

'Several times.' She knew she couldn't allow herself to be seduced by the sensual promise in his voice, at least, not yet. 'Sergio—I…I have decided to marry you.'

Sergio smiled widely, revealing his white teeth. 'Fantastic!' He felt elated. He had spent the past few weeks trying to win Kristen's trust without putting her under pressure, and it seemed that his patience had paid off. 'I'm glad that you want to be my wife, *cara*.'

He wanted to sweep her into his arms and carry her off to bed so that they could celebrate by making love. He had missed her like hell while he had been away and the news that she was ready to commit herself to him suggested that she had missed him too. Although she had not actually said so. Sergio's elation dimmed a little as doubt crept into his mind. Kristen had said that Nico had missed him when he had gone to Hong Kong, but she had made no reference to *her* feelings.

'It will be good for Nico to grow up with both his parents,' he murmured. 'I'm glad we have been able to resolve matters without a judge having to decide who should have custody of him.'

'Y…yes,' she agreed faintly. Sergio's words were an unwelcome reminder that he had been prepared to fight her for custody of Nico, an unwelcome reminder that the only reason he had asked her to marry him was because he wanted his son. Kristen's determination to admit her love for him faltered. 'Of course our marriage will be for Nico's sake,' she said quickly. 'He adores you, and he is so happy living here in Sicily. I've realised that it would be unfair of me to take him back to London. Also…' a soft flush stained her cheeks '…I think it would be nice for him to have a brother or sister. He's three, and already there will be a big age gap between him and another child, even if I fell pregnant straight away.'

A lead weight settled in the pit of Sergio's stomach. Why did he feel so damnably disappointed that Kristen's reasons for deciding to marry him were sensible and coldly logical? he asked himself irritably. Four years ago he had sensed that she had been falling in love with him, and he had hoped over the past weeks that he might have revived her feelings for him. The realisation that she regarded him as a stud was bitterly hurtful.

He lifted his hand and released the mother-of-pearl clip that secured her chignon so that her hair fell like a curtain of gold silk around her shoulders. 'It would make sense for us to get married as soon as possible. What kind of wedding would you like?'

Taken aback by his cool, almost indifferent tone, Kristen shrugged helplessly. 'Nothing fancy. After all, we're not marrying for conventional reasons so it would be silly to go to a lot of fuss. Maybe we could just slip off to a register office.'

Sergio's brows rose. 'Can you clarify what you mean by "conventional reasons"?'

'Well, it's not as though we are in love with each other like most couples are when they decide to marry…is it?' she said huskily. 'It's just a sensible arrangement.'

'Indeed it is,' Sergio agreed pleasantly. His eyes were hooded, but Kristen sensed that for some inexplicable reason, he was angry with her. 'So, following on the sensible theme, I assume you hope to fall pregnant quickly so that Nico can have a little playmate?'

She bit her lip. 'Well…yes.'

'In that case, we'd better have sex.'

Kristen caught her breath as he swung her round and briskly ran the zip of her dress down her spine. With no straps to hold it up, the taffeta gown slithered to the floor and for some silly reason she was tempted to cover her breasts with her hands when he spun her back to face him. She couldn't explain why she felt so vulnerable. He was the same man who had made love to her with tender passion these past weeks, yet tonight his smile did not reach his eyes and his calculating expression chilled her.

'You had better get into bed—unless you want me to take you here on the carpet?'

'Sergio…?' She couldn't disguise the tremor in her voice but, before she could ask him why he was acting this way, his head swooped and he slanted his mouth over hers, kissing her with searing passion that lit a flame inside her so that she wound her arms around his neck as he lifted her and carried her over to the bed. He placed her on the silk bedspread and she watched dry-mouthed while he stripped down to his underwear. His boxers followed his trousers to the floor and, as usual, the sight of his jutting arousal turned her insides to marshmallow. But, instead of stretching out next to her and taking her in his arms as she hoped he would do, he tugged her knickers off and pushed her legs apart.

Anticipation licked through her as he cupped her breasts and rolled her nipples between his fingers until they hardened and tingled. She was on fire for him, but the faintly speculative expression in his eyes disturbed her.

'Sergio, is something wrong?'

'What could possibly be wrong, *cara*?' he drawled. 'We've both got what we want, especially if you conceive a child tonight.'

If all she wanted was a stud, that was what she would get, Sergio thought grimly. He didn't want to admit that she had hurt more than his pride. His heart was hurting, and that made him angry because he didn't want to feel vulnerable. He didn't want to feel anything, certainly not this hollow ache of loneliness.

He slid his hands beneath her bottom, tilted her hips and unhesitatingly drove his hard shaft into her. Kristen had been fantasising about him making love to her all evening and her body was eager and receptive. But Sergio stilled.

'Did I hurt you?' He cursed roughly. 'I should have taken more care.'

He began to withdraw, but Kristen wrapped her arms around his neck and pulled him back down. 'You didn't hurt me.' Casting aside her pride, she whispered, 'Make love to me, Sergio, please…'

Her husky plea breached Sergio's defences and, with a low groan, he thrust into her and felt the sweet embrace of her body as her vaginal muscles tightened around him. Something was happening to him. He no longer felt in control of himself, but after a lifetime of controlling his emotions he was afraid to let go. Instead he concentrated on giving Kristen physical pleasure. He knew how to please her, knew every secret of her body, and he made love to her with all his skill while he desperately tried to keep his mind, his soul detached from her.

Kristen sensed that something was different. There was no tenderness in the way Sergio made love to her, but her body did not care and simply responded to his mastery so that too soon she felt the first spasms of her orgasm and she gave a soft cry as indescribable pleasure overwhelmed her and enslaved her in its sensual embrace.

Sergio must have been deliberately pacing himself until he felt her come and before the ripples of her climax had faded he gave a powerful thrust and spilled his seed into her, but his harsh groan seemed to have been torn from his throat and almost immediately he rolled off her.

She lay beside him, stunned by the swift, almost emotionless coupling they had just shared. She didn't know what to say to him, especially when he murmured, 'I hope I satisfied you, *cara*?' The endearment sounded faintly mocking and her hurt turned to anger. She wanted to demand what the hell was wrong with him, but he had already got up from the bed and was pulling on his trousers and his grim expression warned her that a confrontation between them now would be explosive.

'I need to read through some paperwork in connection with the phone call I took earlier. I'll go downstairs to my study and leave you to get some sleep.' He hesitated, and for a second she glimpsed a look of pain in his eyes that tugged on her heart. But he blinked, and she wondered if she had imagined it as he said in a curiously husky voice, 'It was a tiring day.'

It had been a perfect day that had been ruined by Sergio's sudden change of mood. Hours later, Kristen was still awake, trying to understand what had gone wrong that had turned him into a cold stranger. Maybe he had changed his mind and no longer wanted to marry her? But he wanted Nico, and so had decided he would have to go through with a wedding to gain custody of his son.

She had promised herself she would not cry, but alone in the bed they usually shared she couldn't hold back her tears. When Sergio stood beside the bed a little before dawn and watched her while she slept, the sight of her tear-streaked face made his gut twist. He reached down and touched her hair. He longed to slide between the sheets and draw her into his arms, but he couldn't tonight after the cold way he had made love to her. It was not her fault that she did not love him. *Dio*, his own mother had not loved him, so why should anyone else? he thought despairingly. He despised himself for upsetting Kristen tonight. She had been right to be wary of him and he couldn't blame her if tomorrow she told him she had changed her mind about marrying him.

His throat ached, and he dashed his hand across his eyes. Big boys don't cry, he reminded himself derisively. He had learned that lesson when he had been only a few years older than Nico, but as he stumbled into the sitting room and sank down onto a chair his shoulders shook with the storm force of his emotions.

Sergio wasn't lying next to her in bed when Kristen woke up. She hadn't really expected him to be, but the sight of the empty space on the pillow instead of his silky, sleep-rumpled hair intensified the empty feeling inside her. Fortunately Nico hurtled into the room like a small tornado and, by focusing on getting him washed and dressed and ready for breakfast, she was able to put her misery in a box, to be dealt with later. It was something she'd had plenty of practice doing after she had left Sicily four years ago, she thought ruefully. But this time around running away wasn't an option. She had to put Nico's best interests first, and that undoubtedly meant remaining at Casa Camelia.

When she went downstairs the butler informed her that Sergio had gone to Rome and would not be back until late that evening. Kristen knew that the Castellano Group's head office was located in the capital city. She understood that Sergio held an important position in the company but, while she could cope with her own disappointment that he would be away all day, it was not fair on Nico. Her old fear that he would become bored of fatherhood and return to his old workaholic ways was still on her mind that afternoon when she took Nico up to La Casa Bianca to visit his grandfather.

Tito was in the garden, resting beneath the shade of a pergola. Age and poor health had etched deep lines on his face, but his eyes lit up as he watched Nico kicking a football across the lawn.

'My grandson is a fine boy and a true Castellano. He reminds me of his father when he was a child.' His voice became husky. 'But I do not have many memories of Sergio. He was very young when my wife took him away, and when I saw him again he was almost a man.'

Kristen bit her lip, startled by the emotion she had heard in Tito's voice. 'Did you miss him during the ten years that he was living in America?'

'With all my heart.' Tito sighed deeply. 'I desperately wanted to bring him home to Sicily, but his mother told me that he was happy living with her and didn't want to come back to me. I feared that Patti had poisoned his mind against me. But what could I do? If I had snatched him back he might have hated being here, and hated me. And so I waited and hoped that one day he would return. But every time I looked at his twin brother it was a painful reminder that I had two sons, and when Sergio did finally come home there was a distance between us that I have never been able to breach.'

'Have you ever told him what you have just told me?' Kristen said in a choked voice. 'Because, if not, I think you should as soon as possible. Sergio's childhood growing up with his mother was…difficult,' she said carefully, not sure how much Tito knew about the abuse Sergio had suffered as a little boy. 'He believes that you didn't love him, and that was why you didn't try to regain custody of him.' She stared at the elderly man, her eyes bright with tears. 'Please talk to him and let him know that you did— and do—care about him. It…it could make all the difference to how he feels about himself.'

Tito nodded slowly. 'Castellano men are not good at showing their emotions.' He darted a keen glance at her. 'But perhaps you have discovered this?' He sighed again. 'I am old, and I would like to set the record straight with my son while I still have time.'

'Thank you,' Kristen whispered fervently.

'You love him, don't you?' Tito smiled gently at her

startled expression. 'I saw your love for him in your eyes the first day when you introduced me to my grandson. And I also saw that Sergio loves you.'

Kristen's heart jolted beneath her ribs. She was tempted to tell Tito he was mistaken, but what was the point in shattering an old man's dreams? Instead, she called to Nico, who had kicked his football into a flower bed. 'I think I had better take your grandson home before he completely wrecks the garden,' she said to Tito. She hesitated, hoping he would keep his promise to share his feelings with Sergio. 'Remember what I told you.'

His tired eyes suddenly twinkled. 'And you remember what I told you, my dear.'

CHAPTER TWELVE

KRISTEN WAS LOST in her thoughts as she walked down the front steps of La Casa Bianca and almost collided with a tall, dark figure. For a split second she thought it was Sergio and her pulse quickened, but it slowed again when she saw it was Salvatore.

'Your disappointed expression is not good for my ego,' he teased in the faintly sardonic tone Kristen had come to expect from him. There was an air of remoteness about Sergio's twin brother that she had initially found off-putting. But as she had got to know Salvatore a little better over the past weeks she sensed that he was haunted by the accident three years ago in which his wife had died, and she recognised the same loneliness in him that she sensed in Sergio.

'You took me by surprise. Sergio has gone to Rome for the day,' she said, unaware of the wistful note in her voice.

Salvatore nodded. 'The company's Chief Financial Officer, who is an old family friend, has suffered a suspected heart attack and Sergio has gone to the hospital.' His eyes narrowed on Kristen's pale face. 'I understand that congratulations are in order. My brother told me that the two of you have decided to get married. I expect you are busy planning the wedding?'

Kristen gave a listless shrug. 'It will only be a small

event. After all, it is Sergio's second wedding.' The demon jealousy inside her prompted her to ask, 'Was his wedding to Annamaria an extravagant affair?'

Salvatore looked puzzled. 'Certainly a great event was planned, and Annamaria was thoroughly involved in the preparations. But by the time of the wedding…' He broke off and gave Kristen an intent look. 'I assumed Sergio had told you about Annamaria.'

'He tried,' Kristen admitted. 'But I didn't want to talk about her.' She flushed beneath Salvatore's speculative gaze.

'Take my advice and ask him about her,' he said in an unexpectedly gentle voice that played havoc with Kristen's already raw emotions. The sound of a helicopter overhead caused them both to look towards the sky. 'Sergio is back earlier than expected.' He glanced over to where Nico was playing on the front lawn with Rosa. 'The children are having fun together. Let me take Nico back to the castle so that they can carry on with their game. It will leave you free to have a conversation with my brother, who, by the way, is a damned idiot,' Salvatore muttered. 'I would very much like you to be my sister-in-law, Kristen, and I am looking forward to the wedding.'

The memory of how Sergio had made love to her with such cold detachment the previous night made Kristen feel reluctant to face him and, instead of heading straight back to the villa, she took the path that circled the lake and watched two white swans drifting gracefully on the water. She had read somewhere that swans mated for life. Presumably their lives were less complicated than humans'—but perhaps she was making things complicated when actually the situation was very simple. She sighed. The truth was she loved Sergio and she wanted to spend the rest of her life with him. So why hadn't she told him? If only she had been honest about her feelings for him four years ago; Nico might have grown up with his father from birth. But back then she had been too unsure of herself to fight for what she wanted. Was she going to make the same mistake again? Kristen asked herself impatiently. She didn't have to think about the answer, and she half ran back to Casa Camelia.

The helicopter was on the helipad at the front of the house but there was no sign of Sergio. She raced through the front door and up the stairs, but when she burst into their bedroom she stopped dead when she saw him sitting on the end of the bed. His shoulders were hunched and he was holding his head in his hands, but he lowered them when he heard her and jerked his eyes to her face.

'Where the hell have you been?' he demanded hoarsely. 'You left my father's house nearly an hour ago. I thought...' He swallowed convulsively and, to Kristen's shock, he dashed his hand across his eyes—but not before she had seen the betraying glimmer of moisture on his lashes.

'What did you think?' she asked faintly.

'That you had gone. That I had driven you away.'

Understanding dawned. 'Salvatore took Nico to the castle to play with Rosa. There was no need for you to worry. I wouldn't take Nico away from you,' she told him urgently.

'I wasn't worried about that. I was scared that I had lost *you*.' Sergio stood up and, as he walked towards her, Kristen was shaken by the terrible bleakness in his eyes.

'Would you care if you had lost me?'

'*Dio*, how can you ask that?' His voice shook. 'Of course I would care.' He raked a hand through his hair. 'Perhaps these will explain better than words.'

Only then did Kristen notice the exquisite bouquet of

red roses on her dressing table. *What on earth?* She bit her lip as Sergio handed the bouquet to her. The sensual fragrance of the roses filled her senses and her fingers trembled as she stroked the velvet-soft petals. There was a note attached to the bouquet. She ripped it open and stared at Sergio's distinctive bold handwriting:

'Can you ever forgive me?'

He had written one short line, yet she sensed powerful emotion behind the words and it was as if a fog around her brain had suddenly cleared.

What was he asking her to forgive him for? Her throat ached with tears. For finding it hard to show his feelings, or for hiding his emotions, as he had learned to do when he was a child and his mother had beaten him? Dear heaven, she had been so selfish to hide how she felt about him while she waited for him to tell her that he loved her. Maybe he didn't, but he cared about her enough to buy her roses.

'When I arrived home I came to find you to give you the flowers,' he said in a curiously strained voice, 'but one of the staff told me you were visiting my father.'

'I saw the helicopter. Salvatore told me you had gone to the hospital in Rome to visit a friend, but you are back earlier than expected.'

'Fortunately, Gilberto's health scare turned out not to be a heart attack.'

Kristen breathed in the roses' rich perfume. 'These are beautiful. Thank you.'

'*Can* you forgive me for the way I behaved last night, Krissie?'

This was a Sergio she did not recognise. A man clearly wracked with emotion. But what did it mean? What had he meant when he had said he had been afraid he had lost her?

'Sergio…you once offered to tell me about your first

marriage.' She took a deep breath. 'Will you tell me about Annamaria now?'

He frowned, clearly surprised by her request.

'I was desperately hurt when I discovered that you had married so soon after I left Sicily,' Kristen confessed.

'You don't have to remind me that I failed you badly four years ago,' he said harshly. 'It's pathetic, I know, but the truth is I couldn't face up to how I felt about you. It was easier to keep my emotions locked away. I missed you like hell when you left me, but then I heard the news about Annamaria and she became the focus of my attention.

'Annamaria was my best friend,' Sergio continued. 'When I returned to Sicily as a teenager I was full of anger and resentment against my mother, my father and the whole world. Annamaria's father was a close friend of Tito's, and we spent a lot of time together. She saw past my anger, and she was the only person I was able to talk to about how my mother had mistreated me.

'When she was in her early twenties, Annamaria was diagnosed with leukaemia. For eight years she fought the disease, but each time she appeared to be cured it returned. She was in Switzerland to try a new form of treatment during the summer that you came to Sicily. She came home soon after you had left, having learned that her illness was terminal.'

Kristen drew a sharp breath. 'How terrible that must have been for her and her family—and for you.'

'Her father broke the news to me. He also confided that Annamaria's deepest regret was that she would never be a bride and her father would never have the chance to give his only daughter away in a traditional wedding service.'

'I loved Annamaria as a friend.' Sergio sought Kristen's gaze and she saw a plea for understanding in his dark eyes. 'After all the help she had given me, I wanted to make her last months of life as happy as possible, and so I asked her to marry me.'

A gentle smile crossed his face. 'Planning her wedding day gave her something to think about other than her illness. There was the dress, the bridesmaids' outfits, the flowers to organise. We had planned to marry in the village church, with a huge reception afterwards. But Annamaria's health suddenly deteriorated and she was admitted to a hospice. We held the service at her bedside, and she still managed to wear her bridal gown.' He glanced over at the photograph on the desk. 'She looked beautiful. She was so happy that her hair had grown back once she had stopped the chemotherapy. Annamaria was my dear friend and an incredibly brave person,' Sergio said quietly. 'She died five days after our wedding.'

Kristen swallowed hard. 'I'm so sorry. At least you helped her realise her dream.' She wanted to put her arms around Sergio and hug him tight, but she felt ashamed of the jealousy she had felt for Annamaria and she could not meet his gaze.

Where did they go from here? she wondered as the silence lengthened between them. Where was her courage when she needed it? She cleared her throat. 'Sergio, I...'

'Don't,' he interrupted her in a tortured voice. 'Please don't tell me that you have decided not to marry me. I know I deserve it after last night, but will you give me a chance to explain why I behaved like a complete boor?'

When she did not reply, Sergio took a deep breath. 'I never thought I would marry again after Annamaria. I was sure I did not want a wife or a family of my own. Children need to be loved, but I had buried my emotions for so long that I assumed I would not be able to love a child.

'I was wrong,' he said huskily. 'From the moment I met my son I was overwhelmed with love for him. Nico unlocked the key to my heart and showed me that I was capable of love. It was a revelation, but still I was afraid to admit how I felt about you.'

Kristen's heart skittered when he reached out and touched her hair. His hand was unsteady as he slid it beneath her chin and tilted her face to his, and when she looked into his eyes she was stunned by the fierce emotion that he did not try to hide.

'Four years ago I should have listened to my heart, which insisted that you loved me,' he said deeply. 'Instead, I was swayed by the ugly voice inside my head which taunted that if my own mother had not loved me, why should you. Full of bitterness, I remained in Sicily and concentrated on the only thing I seemed to be good at, which was brokering business deals and making money.'

His eyes grew bleak. 'If I had not been in London on a business trip and you had not come to the Hotel Royale, I would never have known about my son. I don't blame you for hiding him from me and I understand why you did. I had shut you out and never shared my emotions with you, and you were scared I would hurt Nico like I had hurt you.'

No one could accuse Sergio of not sharing his emotions now, Kristen thought. Her heart ached as she stared at his haggard face. But she still could not quite believe what her heart was telling her. She had hoped for so long, but maybe her mind was playing tricks.

'After we had slept together at the hotel you only looked for me because you wanted me to make a statement to the press and deny the story they had published about us,' she reminded him.

'That's wasn't the only reason.' Sergio held her gaze. 'I wanted to see you again. The truth is I couldn't stay away from you, Krissie. But I admit that at that point I only hoped to persuade you to resume our affair. I didn't know…I didn't realize…' He hesitated, and in the silence Kristen was sure he must be able to hear the frantic thud of her heart.

'What didn't you realise?' she whispered.

'That I love you.'

Her heart stood still, but she was afraid to believe him. 'You were angry that I had hidden Nico from you.'

'At first, but I soon understood why you had decided to bring him up on your own. I had failed you when you had the miscarriage and let you think I did not want the baby we had lost. It wasn't surprising that you believed I would not want Nico. I was a coward then…and I am still acting like a coward now,' Sergio muttered.

'What do you mean?'

Instead of replying, he strode across the room and opened the drawer in his bedside table. 'I have something that I want to give you, something that might explain my feelings better than I seem to be doing with words.' He walked back to her, holding a small square box, and Kristen caught her breath when he opened the lid and revealed an exquisite oval sapphire surrounded by glittering diamonds.

'I…I don't understand.' The ring was clearly an engagement ring, but she didn't dare accept what her head and the expression in Sergio's eyes were telling her.

'It's very simple,' he said softly. 'I love you, Kristen. Four years ago I refused to admit that I felt anything for you and told myself I only wanted you as my mistress. But I never forgot you, and when I saw you at the Hotel Royale I knew I wanted you back in my life. But then I met Nico, and all my doubts returned. I reasoned that you would not have kept my son from me if you had cared for me.'

'I did care for you,' Kristen broke in, her voice cracking as a tear slid down her cheek. 'I loved you with all my heart. Last night I wanted to tell you…' Seeing him frown at her use of the past tense, she flung her arms around him and held him as though she would never ever let go. 'I wanted to tell you that I still love you and I never stopped. But I lost my nerve, and then…you were so cold.'

'Krissie…*tesoro*,' Sergio groaned. 'I was disappointed that you had only agreed to marry me because you wanted a brother or sister for Nico.'

'And I thought the only reason you asked me marry you was because you wanted your son.'

He shook his head and threaded his fingers through her hair. 'It was always you, my golden girl. Having Nico is a bonus. You are the love of my life—' his voice roughened '—but I was afraid to tell you and risk being rejected.'

As he had been rejected by his mother, and believed he had been rejected by his father, Kristen thought emotionally. 'You need to have a chat with Tito,' she murmured.

'What I need to do is make love to the woman who is very soon going to become my wife,' he said firmly, suddenly all dominant Sicilian male. But he kissed her with a tender passion that brought tears to Kristen's eyes, and her heart turned over when she saw that his lashes were wet.

'I will never stop loving you,' she said urgently, desperate to dispel the faint shadows still lingering in his eyes. 'You, me and Nico, and any other children we might have, we will be the family you never had. And, when we are old and grey, our grandchildren will hope that they find love as deep and long-lasting as the love we share for each other.'

Sergio did not reply. He could not when he was so choked with the emotions that he had held inside him for so long. But he told Kristen in myriad other ways how much he loved her. He claimed her lips in a sensuous kiss that made them both tremble. And when he undressed her and stroked his hands possessively over her breasts and stomach before moving lower to slip between her thighs, his gentle caresses spoke of a love that would last for all time.

'*Ti amo,*' he whispered against her lips as he made love to her with exquisite care. And the words healed him, completed him and left him with a deep sense of peace because he knew that Kristen loved him.

They married two weeks later in the little chapel on the Castellano estate. Kristen wore a simple white silk gown decorated with crystals on the bodice, and the garland of pink rosebuds in her hair matched the exquisite bouquet of roses that Sergio had placed on the bed on the morning of the wedding, while she had been getting dressed. The attached note simply read: '*I love you*' but those three words meant everything to Kristen. Sergio's unhappy childhood had made him suppress his emotions and he couldn't change overnight. But he was determined Kristen would never have reason to doubt that she was his sun and Nico was his moon. And knowing that his love was returned gave him the confidence to share his feelings.

Nico was an adorable pageboy and his cousin Rosa was a pretty flower-girl. The wedding was a glorious, happy occasion and even Salvatore, who had the role of Sergio's best man, gave one of his rare smiles when the groom kissed his bride in front of the congregation of family and friends in the chapel.

'I wish your brother could fall in love and be as happy as we are,' Kristen said to her new husband as they stood on the steps of the chapel for photographs.

'I wish so too. But I don't think any man could be as happy as I am,' Sergio told her in an unsteady voice. He drew her into his arms and looked into her eyes, which were as blue as the summer sky above them. 'You are my wife, my lover, my best friend and the love of my life, and I am the luckiest man in the world.'

Kristen blinked hard. 'I am the luckiest woman, and I'm so happy that I'm going to cry,' she said huskily.

'I love you, Krissie,' Sergio murmured against her cheek as he caught a tear on his lips. And then he kissed her with such tender passion, such love, that no words were needed.

* * * * *

Wrap up warm this winter with Sarah Morgan...

Sleigh Bells in the Snow

Kayla Green loves business and hates Christmas.

So when Jackson O'Neil invites her to Snow Crystal Resort to discuss their business proposal... the last thing she's expecting is to stay for Christmas dinner. As the snowflakes continue to fall, will the woman who doesn't believe in the magic of Christmas finally fall under its spell...?

4th October

www.millsandboon.co.uk/sarahmorgan

She's loved and lost — will she ever learn to open her heart again?

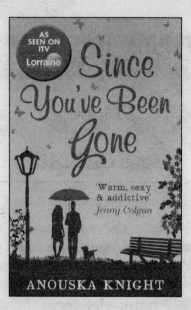

From the winner of ITV Lorraine's Racy Reads, Anouska Knight, comes a heart-warming tale of love, loss and confectionery.

'The perfect summer read — warm, sexy and addictive!'
—Jenny Colgan

For exclusive content visit:
www.millsandboon.co.uk/anouskaknight